Chesapeake
Charlie
and the
STOLEN
DIAMOND

Chesapeake Charlie and the STOLEN DIAMOND

WILLIAM L. COLEMAN

BETHANY HOUSE PUBLISHERS
Minneapolis, Minnesota 55438
A Division of Bethany Fellowship, Inc.

Chesapeake Charlie and the Stolen Diamond
William L. Coleman

Library of Congress Catalog Card Number 81-68077

ISBN 0-87123-170-0

Published by Bethany House Publishers
A Division of Bethany Fellowship, Inc.
6820 Auto Club Road, Minneapolis, Minnesota 55438

Printed in the United States of America

About the Author

WILLIAM L. COLEMAN is a graduate of the Washington Bible College in Washington, D.C., and Grace Theological Seminary in Winona Lake, Indiana. He has pastored three churches: a Baptist Church in Michigan, a Mennonite Church in Kansas, and an Evangelical Free Church in Aurora, Nebraska. He is a Staley Foundation Lecturer. The author of some seventy-five magazine articles, his by-line has appeared in *Christianity Today, Eternity, Campus Life*, and several other Christian magazines. Coleman is best known for his devotional books for children. He is the father of three and makes his home in Nebraska.

Other books in this series

Chesapeake Charlie and the Bay Bank Robbers
Chesapeake Charlie and Blackbeard's Treasure
Chesapeake Charlie and the Haunted Ship

Chapter One

"What's that gizmo?" Kerry asked, looking at the black object.

"A special telescope I've just built," Charlie Dean replied as he stuffed its purple, felt cover into his pocket. He pointed the object toward the sky and held it close to his eye. "That must be our closest star."

"You can't see stars in the daytime, bunkerhead."

"Maybe you're not as smart as you think," Charlie said calmly, still peering into the heavens.

"Let's go. Recess is almost over." Kerry began to walk toward the school building.

"I think that's the Big Dipper—yes, it looks like it."

Kerry's steps slowed. "This is probably some dumb joke like the time you told me I could hear phone conversations by putting my ear against the pole."

"I was just kidding then," replied Charlie.

"The policeman sure laughed. He wanted to know why I was hugging a telephone pole."

"That was different. I've worked hard on this and it has paid off. I see stars."

"I know I'm going to be sorry for this, but let me see."

"Nope—no skeptics."

"Don't play games." Kerry seized the short telescope and aimed it at the sky. "I don't see anything except sky and clouds.

"Hold it closer to your eye."

Kerry pressed the object snuggly against his face.

"What're you guys up to?" Laura's curiosity drew her over to her two friends. "Don't tell me you're bird watching."

"Just buzz off," said Kerry. "I don't see a thing yet, Charlie."

"Turn the scope to focus," Charlie suggested.

Kerry rotated the telescope and held it tightly against his eye.

"Not one star."

"Try your left eye," Charlie said.

Kerry obeyed.

"Nothing—I knew it."

"Turn it some more," Charlie insisted.

Kerry finally removed the scope from his face. "I don't see anything."

Laura giggled and clapped her hand to her mouth.

"Don't pay any attention to her," said Charlie with a wide smile. "Try your other eye again. Hold the scope tightly and turn it."

Kerry reluctantly tried again.

Laura burst into laughter as he lifted the scope.

"Hey, guys!" Laura yelled toward a group of students. "Come quick!" She started to laugh again.

Four or five friends gathered, stared at Kerry and burst into laughter.

"Maybe—maybe," Charlie could barely hold back a laugh, "we should try this some other time." He retrieved the telescope, put it in the purple cover and started across the playground, laughing until he was red in the face.

"I knew it was a trick," Kerry muttered. "What's so funny?"

"Let's go in and get my purse. I'll show you," Laura said with a giggle.

Back in the building, Laura handed him a mirror from her purse. The rest of the group howled and roared as Kerry stared at his reflection. Each of his eyes had a large, black circle around it.

"See you, raccoon eyes!" one boy yelled as the bell rang to end recess.

School was a good place to be with friends and pull a few pranks. Studying wasn't a favorite activity, but it was tolerable. Sometimes Charlie wondered why school couldn't be taught outside on the shores of the Chesapeake Bay. He felt there was more to learn and enjoy around Collin's Landing than in all the books a library could hold.

Charlie loved to wake up early and see what new things he could try. Most people seemed to resent autumn. It meant they had to put away their water skis, secure their boats, give up much of their crabbing and try to survive the winter. For Chesapeake Charlie the cool breezes and colorful leaves signaled new adventures. There would be oysters to tong. The beautiful Canada geese would fly in V-formations across the sky and land on the Bay marsh. Winter crabs could be caught by those who had the patience to find them. Ice on the Chesapeake would bring danger and exciting stories of men wrestling against nature.

Even the long winter evenings couldn't discourage Charlie Dean. Inventions simmered in the back of his mind, hobbies needed attention, and pet theories needed testing. With his life already jammed, Charlie had decided to wedge in one more thing. This fall he had acquired a new pet.

"Why did you tell the Hendersons you'd take Arnold?" Pete asked his older brother, Charlie.

"I thought Mom and Dad would let us keep him."

The boys were headed for one of their favorite places: their own backyard. It was cluttered with a couple of rowboats, a shed, and one long clothesline. It was bordered by a wide shoreline facing the beautiful Chesapeake Bay.

Near the Dean house was a white doghouse. When the weather was bad Throckmorton, Charlie's not-so-brave beagle, liked to hide there.

"Somewhere in your mini-mind you imagined that *our* parents would let us keep a *goat*?"

"Not just a goat—a *watch*-goat," Charlie explained.

"A watch-goat! I thought Mom would fall off her chair when you said watch-goat."

"Why not?" Charlie demanded. "If a burglar ever comes, Throckmorton will probably climb a tree or crawl under a boat."

"What are you going to do—teach Arnold to bark?"

"A goat is a triple threat. It can let out a blood-curdling baa, butt and bite. Those're three things Throckmorton won't do."

"Sounds like a real loser to me, Charlie."

The goat was tied to Mrs. Dean's clothesline with a long rope that allowed it to roam and eat grass. Charlie reached over to pet the animal.

"Talk about bad breath," Pete groaned. "He

needs a Listerine bath."

"That's next. We can put him in the old tin laundry tub and scrub him down. Then we'll convince Mom to reconsider."

The boys dragged the laundry tub away from the garage and parked it near the goat. They quickly hooked up a hose and began running water into the tub.

"We've disproved another myth," Charlie announced proudly. "Goats *don't* eat clothing. Look at our wash. He hasn't munched a single thread."

Throckmorton cast a suspicious look at the bony creature. Charlie poured laundry soap into the bath, and Pete added a healthy dose of green mouthwash.

"Here, Arnold," Charlie called, pointing toward the sudsy water. "Here, Arnold." Charlie slapped his hands on his knees and motioned.

"You don't *ask*," Pete scolded. "Goats respect *authority*. Arnold—in the water—now!"

Arnold glanced up from the thick, dark grass, blinked at the tub and resumed eating.

"We'll have to use some persuasion," Charlie said.

Both boys marched over to the animal and searched for a place to grab. Pete tried to lift Arnold's hind legs.

"Ouch!" he shouted as Arnold crashed a hoof onto Pete's foot.

Meanwhile Charlie wrestled with the goat's head. Arnold thrust his short horns at Charlie and kept him from taking a firm hold. Finally, Charlie locked an arm under the animal's chin.

"I've got him! I've got him!" Charlie yelled.

"I can't pick up this right leg," Pete responded.

Rip! Thump!

Charlie crashed to the ground.

"Are you all right?" Pete called as he tightly held Arnold's left leg.

Charlie looked up to see Arnold chewing a piece of blue denim.

"He's got my pocket. That goat's eating my front pocket!"

Charlie struggled to his feet and grabbed Arnold's collar. Pete pushed against Arnold's bony hips, and the stubborn goat moved sideways.

"He's moving!" Charlie shouted. "Quit it, you weirdo." Arnold had locked his teeth onto Charlie's jacket sleeve and was beginning to chew.

The two boys were edging the goat nearer to his bathtub. Charlie's sleeve seemed to act as a pacifier to keep Arnold's mind busy.

"A few more feet," groaned Pete.

"Hurry, my sleeve is tearing." They had managed to get Arnold next to the tub, broadside.

"There, let's lift him," said Pete.

"On three."

"One."

"Two."

Sploosh!

Arnold had shaken his head and hurled Charlie headfirst into the cold suds. With two shakes of his rump, Arnold knocked Pete loose. The startled boy tottered. He waved his hands frantically trying to gain his balance.

"A-a-a-h!" Pete collapsed into the cold water, and cold white soap bubbles fluffed into the air.

The goat trotted smuggly away.

Shivering and sputtering, Charlie and Pete clambered out of the water.

"Why did you let go?" demanded Pete.

"*Me* let go? He *flipped* me."

"I agree with Mom. Sell the beast—give him away if you have to." Pete growled as the soggy duo trudged toward the house.

"Don't give up so soon. I've got a great idea."

"What are you doing?" Laura yelled. "You can't hang that goat! I'll call the police!" She waved her hands wildly as she entered the backyard.

"Keep it down," Charlie pleaded. "We're not hanging anybody."

A rope hung over a large tree limb. Pete held one end while Charlie tied the other under Arnold's chest and hips.

"We have to give Arnold a bath so my folks will let us keep him."

The limb stretched over the tub. Arnold stood on an over-turned rowboat, munching a bucketful of grass.

"You just watch." Charlie tightened the knot behind Arnold's front legs.

"We're going to swing Arnold out over the pool," Pete volunteered.

"And then drop him gently into his waiting bath," Charlie added. "Watch closely as geniuses go to work—better back up."

"Keep the rope tight," Charlie commanded.

"Roger."

"Prepare to launch."

"Roger."

"Launch!"

Charlie shoved Arnold in the side and sent him sprawling off the boat. However, Arnold's hooves remained on the ground. Charlie pushed and grunted.

"Pull, Pete!"

"I'm trying, I'm trying!"

Pete could barely hold onto the rope. Arms stretched high above his head, Pete was standing on his toes.

"Don't let go!" Charlie shouted as he stumbled back and forth across the yard, fighting to push Arnold off the ground. The bewildered goat whirled about and bleated loudly.

"Hurry!" Pete pleaded.

"Lift him!"

"Ba-a-a!"

"I'm trying!"

"More!"

"Ba-a-a!" Pete balanced desperately on his tiptoes, his body stretched like a drum; Charlie chased the fleet-footed Arnold, trying to give him a lift. Laura held her sides as she laughed, trying to keep her ribs from cracking.

"Bring him closer to the tree!" Pete screeched.

"Give me more rope!"

"I can't hold on!"

"I've almost got him there."

"My arms are coming off!"

Throckmorton was now galloping around the yard barking and yelping. He ran dizzily between Charlie and Pete, not sure how to play the game. Laura finally dropped on a lawn chair and tried to stop laughing so that she could breathe.

Bong.

The sound echoed across the yard as Charlie's head crashed into the clothesline post. He fell backward like a dead tree. The goat whirled and galloped toward Pete. The sudden slack in the rope sent him off balance and he sprawled across the grass.

Laura jumped to her feet and gasped, afraid both boys had broken into pieces. Her sympathy disappeared quickly as they struggled to stand up, moaning loudly.

"You big cement-heads," roared Laura. It wasn't her normal laugh. This one rang with a most insulting sound.

"Outsmarted by a goat!" she bellowed. "Your parents had better build cages to protect you two!"

"They're coming!" called Mr. Dean. Charlie's father focused his binoculars which were aimed toward the evening sky.

It had been a few hours since Charlie had collided with the post, but his head was still throbbing.

"The geese are beautiful," Mr. Dean continued.

A flock of Canada geese is one of many majestic sights that paint the Chesapeake skies every fall. Each autumn the "honkers" leave their home near the Ungava Peninsula in Quebec and migrate south. Their V-formations stream steadily into the Bay area, providing one of nature's amazing displays.

"I knew it," said Charlie. "I just knew it. The rains and a south wind do it everytime. After it rains the wind shifts and in come the geese."

Charlie's excitement restored the bounce in his step and made his headache seem far away. His father handed him the glasses for a closer look.

Ronk-a ronk-ronk. Ronk-a ronk-ronk.

Charlie loved all of it—the honk of Canada geese ringing in his ears, the brackish smell of the Bay flooding his nostrils, and the gentle fall breeze fluttering through his hair. It seemed like paradise on earth.

"They're landing, Dad; they're landing!"

Using the binoculars, Charlie watched the geese descend onto the marsh. Nearly a dozen made a wide turn, stopped flapping their wings and spread them like umbrellas. The geese glided onto the water like feathers.

"Canada geese really love the Bay," Mr. Dean commented.

"Let's bring your camera next time and take pictures," said Charlie.

"We should get plenty of chances. Thousands of them will flock here—probably half a million."

"You'd think that with so many houses being built along the waterfront, the geese would be scared off."

"Hardly. More are landing here each year. There must be three, maybe four times as many geese here as there used to be."

"Won't they run out of food?"

"Not in the Chesapeake; it's full of natural food. There also seems to be a lot of grain left in the fields. The Bay is like a huge free restaurant for geese."

"There's a white-haired old lady standing on the shore," Charlie noted as he peered through the glasses. "She seems to be calling the geese toward her and throwing some bread on the water."

"Not much chance they'll come—they're shy of people. She must be a tourist."

"Is it all right if some of us go tonging for oysters in the morning since tomorrow's Saturday?" Charlie asked as he and his father started back toward the house.

"Sure. I'll need you for a couple hours in the afternoon for chores, but the morning will be fine." Mr. Dean started to wrap his arm around Charlie's shoulders and then drew back.

"Do you smell something?" Mr. Dean asked as his nose wrinkled.

"What do you mean?"

"Well. . ." Mr. Dean stepped away from his son.

"Oh, that—it's nothing. We were just trying to wash Arnold. I guess I stink a little, huh?"

"I'm not sure 'little' is the right word."

Smack. The screen door on the back porch slammed shut as Charlie's mother stormed into the backyard.

"Where is that goat?" Mrs. Dean asked angrily.

"You mean Arnold—our watch-goat?" asked Charlie.

"Watch, nothing! That garbage disposal has to go."

"He's no trouble—honest, Mom. We almost gave him a bath today."

"He goes, I tell you. Just look at these."

Mrs. Dean held several pieces of cloth in her hand.

"Do you know what these are?"

"Well, uh, not really," Charlie said, hesitating.

"They're the tops of *socks* I had hanging on the line. If you look inside that trashmasher's stomach, I bet you'll find the bottoms. The goat goes."

Chapter Two

Mrs. Dean beamed as she laid a plate of hot oyster sandwiches on the table. "These are great oysters." Charlie's tastebuds danced.

"We got half a bushel," said Charlie. "I could have tonged more if Laura and Kerry hadn't been along."

"Don't brag," cautioned Mrs. Dean as she joined her family for lunch.

"I'm not bragging. Those long tongs almost tear your arms off."

"Let's sing for our prayer," said Mr. Dean.

Charlie liked to sing. He wasn't too concerned about being in tune, but he could belt the words out with gusto. His brother, Pete, wasn't as thrilled with music and mumbled through the song.

"A few of the oysters you caught weren't as good as these in the sandwiches," said Mr. Dean as the four began to eat. He held up a raw oyster in the half shell and showed it to Charlie.

"Notice how puffy this oyster is." Charlie's father pressed down on the raw meat with his table knife. "It's watery and the color is bad."

"Is pollution hurting them?" Charlie asked.

"I don't think that's the main problem. Some people think the oyster population goes in cycles. There certainly aren't as many as there used to be. Maybe we're taking too many out of the Bay and not putting enough back."

"That's exactly it." Charlie considered himself an absolute authority on the Bay. "We need more hatcheries."

"They cost a lot of money," Mr. Dean commented. "I just read in the newspaper today that the department in charge of the seafood hatcheries is going to receive less tax money next year."

"Speaking of the newspaper," Charlie said, "there's a big article on the Ludlow diamond. It's going to be on display in Cambridge next week."

"That's one of the few diamonds ever found in Maryland," said Mr. Dean.

"Where did they find it?" Pete wondered.

"In the Cumberland mountains, of all places," Mrs. Dean answered.

"Did the paper say what it was worth?" Mr. Dean asked.

"At least $50,000," said Charlie. "I'd like to see it. Any chance of us getting over to Cambridge?"

Mr. Dean took a sip of his coffee. "Possibly. Your Uncle wants us to come over to Salisbury and try fishing in Anderson Lake. Please pass the sandwiches. We could maybe stop in Cambridge on the way."

"Hold this." Charlie handed two sets of nylon lines to Laura. The sun was dropping close to the horizon as their rowboat sat quietly on the Bay. There was hardly a ripple to rock them.

"Man, this is living." Charlie pulled two buckets apart. "In the fall you can catch oysters in the morning and late crabs in the evening."

"It's also chilly." Laura pulled up the collar on her red jacket.

"Tie this on the end of your string."

"What in the world is it?"

"Just a new bait."

"I'll use the chicken, thank you."

"You have to be willing to try new things."

"What is this gook? It looks like liver."

"Just tie it on."

"All right—but what is it?"

"Bull's lips."

"What?"

"Bull's lips."

Laura gasped and dropped the bait.

"You animal!"

"What's the matter?"

"You're sick."

"I read about a man who uses bull's lips, so I asked for some from the butcher. Let's try them before you have a fit."

Laura fought back her squeamishness and was soon catching crabs. She and Charlie had soon pulled in a half-dozen jimmies.

"The crabs like the deep water better in the fall." Charlie sounded like a lecturer every now and then. Laura and his other friends had learned to quietly ignore him at such times.

"As the water gets colder they look for warmer areas. The oysters would probably move around, too, if they had legs."

"What do you think about the vote next week?" Laura interrupted, trying to shorten Charlie's speech.

"What vote?"

"The Laotians, rock head. There's more to life than crabs and bull's lips, you know."

"You mean at church?"

"Of course. Do you think we should adopt a Laotian family?" Laura pulled at her line but the crab let go.

"I don't know. My parents think we should—but I hear a lot of rumors about refugees."

"Like what?" Laura peered into the water for any sign of action.

"Some people think foreigners just come over here to get on welfare."

"But that's where our church comes in. We help them find housing and jobs and make sure they learn the language. It sounds exciting to me."

"I think we should move cautiously before we get involved with strangers."

"Sure, but they aren't like creepy kidnappers, driving around in cars giving candy to little kids."

"Laura, for once I think you're probably right. I guess the Bible does say something about helping people in need."

"Especially those in *real* need. Jesus said that when we help someone in need, it's just like helping Him."

"My parents will probably vote for it."

"Here he comes," Laura announced. "He feels like a big one."

"He's huge!" Charlie gasped. "Don't rattle him."

Laura held the net firmly in her right hand while she pulled the line steadily with her left. Any sudden jerk might send her catch scurrying.

"Steady, steady."

"Cool it. You make me nervous."

Laura dipped her net smoothly into the water and eased it under the wiggling crab. Holding her line motionless, she inched the net up until it was just under the creature.

"I've got it! I've got it!" she cried as the net swung up and onto the boat.

"Drop him into the bucket."

"He's climbing out!" she squealed.

The large crab raced up the side of the net and bolted out. He hit the bottom of the boat like a rock and began running.

"Get him!" The barefoot Charlie flew up on the wooden bench.

Smack! Laura sent the net crashing down around the crab. It continued snapping its claws, but the huge jimmie could run no farther.

"Look at him!" Charlie shouted. "Must be the biggest one I've ever seen. Hold on and I'll measure him."

Charlie took a ruler from the bait box. If crabs were smaller than the law allowed, Charlie threw them back. He didn't really enjoy rules, but when it came to the Bay, Charlie cared for it like a loving father.

"Can you believe this?" Charlie pressed his ruler across the crab's back. "It measures eight-and-a-half inches spike tip to spike tip. That's not a record, but man it's close!"

"And I suppose you know what the record is," Laura said sarcastically.

"As a matter of fact, it's a little over nine inches spike to spike. This baby will probably measure nineteen inches from claw to claw."

"Let's get him into the bucket."

Charlie grabbed the animal across the back with a pair of wooden tongs. Gingerly Laura lifted her net as Charlie held their new treasure tightly. Moving as one they shifted toward the bucket and lowered the net to the top.

When Charlie let go, the giant crab clamped tightly to the net strings. After a few well-aimed whacks from the tongs, the crab let go and dropped into the shallow water.

The crab's smaller relatives tried to get away from the giant, but they had no place to go.

Charlie secured an extra net over the bucket top to discourage any escape attempts.

"Wait'll I show everybody what we caught." Charlie could hardly stand still.

"What do you mean, 'we'?"

"Come on. You wouldn't have caught it without my bull's lips."

"Baloney. I didn't even use those creepy lips. Just look at my bait—a trusty old chicken neck. Ha-Ha. I switched back to a *sensible* bait. So let's drop the 'we.' "

"Girls! They want all the credit and none of the work. Let's head for home before it gets any darker."

"Hold it a minute!" Charlie exclaimed. "I've got one on my line. It might be bigger than yours."

Charlie had little difficulty scooping his catch in the net. It was a frisky fighter but not nearly record size.

Suddenly Laura grabbed Charlie's arm. Speechless, she pointed toward an object gliding along the water's surface.

Charlie's jaw dropped as he saw a head and

shoulders moving in their direction. The dark green creature was like nothing he had ever seen before.

They both stiffened as chills ran through their bodies. Charlie swallowed hard. Silently the strange animal continued to approach.

Its head was almost round, and when its mouth opened, jagged teeth gleamed. Large, white eyes peered at the boat while two bulky ears flopped loosely. The creature had a muscular neck.

Charlie and Laura could practically hear their hearts thumping. Their hands were clammy.

Suddenly, the head dropped beneath the surface. Charlie lunged for the oars and began rowing frantically for shore.

"Grab the met and not the hinster!" Charlie cried out.

"What?"

"I said net the grab and minster the hot!" he yelled louder as he rowed with all his strength.

"You mean grab the net and hit the monster?" Laura raised the net high.

"That's what I said!"

The harder Charlie rowed the slower the boat went. Much of the time his oars skimmed the top of the water, accomplishing nothing.

Holding her net high, Laura searched the water for any sight of the mysterious monster. One glimpse and she would crown it.

The evening darkness grew thicker. Laura was now afraid that if the monster did surface, she would not see it in time.

By now Charlie had regained his coordination and the boat was moving smoothly across the Bay. When they arrived at the pier, both Charlie and Laura felt shaky and were glad to be safe. Without looking back they raced for Charlie's house.

"Hold on!" Mr. Dean tried to calm the breathless pair as they stumbled through the back door. "You look as if you've seen someone's ghost."

"Worse than that, Dad, worse than that." Charlie's lips quivered as he spoke.

Kerry snickered as he listened to Charlie's story. They were standing alone in the music room on the third floor.

"I'm sorry I told you. I knew you weren't smart enough to handle this." Charlie was frustrated.

"A monster in the Bay? Charlie, you've gotta be kidding!"

"Ask Laura. She'll tell you."

"Sure, the Chesapeake Lagoon Monster."

"Lots of monsters have been seen in the Bay."

"How do you know?"

"I looked it up."

"Let's forget about the monster. Wouldn't it be funny to toss someone's books out the window? Three floors down to the pavement—b-o-o-m!"

"Don't be childish. Thirty- and forty-foot creatures with green eyes have been sighted in the Bay, and no one has been able to explain it."

"Come on, let's drop Bill's books out the window. He'll just laugh."

"A man fishing on the Choptank one night had something grab his boat. He had to hack its arm off with a hatchet."

"Charlie," Kerry said sternly, "this isn't like you.

You usually stick to the facts."

"This *is* a fact. Ask Laura."

"Have some fun. Let's throw some books out."

"All right. Have it your way."

Smiling broadly, Kerry turned and raised the window.

"Here." Charlie handed Kerry a short stack of school books and a loose-leaf notebook.

Kerry took the stack, laughed devilishly and hurled the books into space.

In less than a second Kerry's glee changed to horror—he was watching his own books plummet toward the ground. They thudded against the concrete sidewalk. Several loose papers fluttered slowly behind. Mr. Rossim, the principal, was coming down the sidewalk. Kerry ducked down, but he was sure he'd been spotted.

The class bell rang. Students poured into the room. Charlie found his chair and grinned like a cat that just ate the canary.

"No one believes me." Charlie kicked a pop can as he walked down the paved road. Throckmorton kept wandering off.

"I only tried once," Laura said glumly. "When I saw the expression on Mom's face, I decided to keep it to myself. I don't want everybody thinking I'm nuts."

"But we did see it, didn't we?" Charlie sounded unsure of himself.

"We certainly saw *something*," answered Laura.

"You'd think someone would believe us."

"Let's face it, Charlie; you've told so many wild

stories that people don't know which ones to believe."

"Sure. But this one really happened."

"I think we'd better drop it."

"If we just had some evidence—something we could show people—like a claw or a tooth print."

"I say forget it."

"There they are." Charlie pointed toward the cottages.

Kerry and Pete were waiting for them. Kerry was clutching a white shoe box and Pete held three balloons and a BB gun.

"Where did you get the three helium balloons?" Charlie asked Pete.

"Kerry got them at the grocery store. They're giving them away this week for some promotion."

"This looks like another weird idea," said Laura.

"Be patient, a genius is at work," insisted Kerry.

"You're going to send secret messages on balloon strings—not very original."

"Just hold your lip. You might learn something."

Kerry carefully lifted a small crab from the box. He held it out toward Charlie. "Grab its claws."

"What are you doing?" a strange voice asked.

The four turned to see an elderly lady peering over their shoulders. Charlie recognized her immediately as the lady who had been calling the geese. He had seen her through his dad's binoculars.

"Just a history-making experiment. Someday armies will use this in warfare," Kerry replied as he tied a balloon string to the crab's body.

"Mind if I watch?" she asked.

"Not at all."

"When the Humane Society finds out, I'll tell them you were the 'genius' behind the plan," Laura assured him.

"Stand back." Holding the squirming crab high with one hand, Kerry lifted his other hand to check the wind. "Just right," he announced.

Kerry released his invention and stepped back to see what would happen. The three balloons floated toward the water. Never rising more than three or four feet above the surface, the shackled crab sailed over the Bay.

"Beautiful, beautiful," said Kerry. "Hand me the gun."

Kerry grabbed the BB gun and aimed.

"Don't hit the crab," Laura warned.

Pop! The first balloon exploded. On the second shot Kerry missed. Pop! The second balloon flew apart. As the crab sank toward the water, Kerry shot the third balloon into pieces.

"It worked! It worked!" Kerry jumped up and down as if he had just won an Olympic gold medal.

"That's it?" asked Laura.

"And that will be used in *warfare*?" Charlie puzzled.

"Can't you see it? The army will tie thousands of crabs to balloons and send them over an enemy fort. Just as they get over the fort the soldiers will shoot out the balloons. Imagine those enemy soldiers dodging all the flying crabs!"

"Do yourself a favor," Charlie said sternly. "Don't talk about this with the school counselor. She might put you out to sea in a padded boat."

"Oh, I think it was a grand idea," the lady interrupted.

"See?" Kerry puffed out his chest.

"New ideas are fantastic," she continued. "I never try to discourage young talent."

"You don't want to encourage this toad," Laura said. "Last year he wanted to build a tunnel through the earth to China."

"Splendid idea—if he could just solve the heat problem. Oh, allow me to introduce myself. I'm Adelie Morgan. I don't mean to poke my nose in, but you four looked as though you were having fun." She pointed. "I've rented that cottage for a month."

"That's great," Kerry assured her.

"Sure thing," added Charlie. "Where are you from?"

"Pittsburgh. The late Mr. Morgan and I lived there for 28 years. Now that I'm alone, I often take off on little trips like this."

"Don't you mind traveling alone?" asked Laura.

"Not really. I enjoy getting to meet people and learning about their local culture. I used to be a schoolteacher so I miss being around young people."

"There's plenty of culture around here—except for Charlie and Kerry," Laura said.

"Yes, and lots of interesting stories," Pete offered.

"You bet." Charlie seemed to be thinking. "Why, the other day Laura and I saw a real monster stick its head out of the Bay—didn't we Laura?"

"I told you, let's forget that."

"Forget it, nothing! We saw it."

"How fascinating," Mrs. Morgan beamed. "I wish I could see some evidence of a monster. It would be thrilling."

"Well, there might be some evidence," said Charlie.

"What evidence?" asked the startled Laura.

"Never mind. We can talk about it later," Charlie answered.

"I'd better go fix something to eat." Mrs. Morgan turned toward her cottage. "Come and see me anytime. I have a full candy bowl in the living room and no one to share it with. What are your names, by the way?"

Charlie spoke instantly. "That's Kerry, this is Laura—she's okay for a girl; this is my brother, Pete, and I'm Charlie Dean—also known as Chesapeake Charlie.

"If you have any questions about the Bay, don't be afraid to ask," Charlie said proudly. "The Maryland state fish is the Rockfish; the capital is *Annapolis*, not Baltimore; people who work on the water are *watermen*, not fishermen."

"Come back as soon as you can," Mrs. Morgan called.

Chapter Three

"The Colts oughta cream the Jets next Sunday," Kerry whispered to Charlie as they sat together in the visual-aid room at school.

"They'd better win or the coach will be out of a job," Charlie said.

"My dad says Baltimore can't get a better quarterback because they don't want to give up the big bucks."

Mrs. Hobson had finished loading the slide projector and the tape player and was ready to begin. She stood at the back of the room holding the remote control.

"I believe you will find the slide presentation very informative," she explained. "It is called, 'Education Among the Indians of the Andes.' "

A soft groan rose from the students as they heard the title. Mrs. Hobson's hearing problem prevented her from detecting most of the noise.

"Pay close attention. There will be a short quiz on this tomorrow."

Charlie and Kerry were sitting close to the front of the room. Restlessly, Charlie straightened himself in his chair and pulled a small object out of his pocket. He hid it snugly under his thumb.

"Beautiful skies await our arrival in the high

mountains crested with thick forest . . ." the tape began. Dutifully, with the sound of each click from the tape, Mrs. Hobson pressed the button to change slides.

Most of the students settled back for a long nap, but Charlie had other plans. About two minutes into the presentation Charlie pushed his thumb down. The object in his hand gave out a robust click.

Innocently Mrs. Hobson changed the slide.

"Our head guide is Manuel." Instead of a person the slide showed a shrunken head.

A few students snickered and others started to wake up.

Click.

"He introduces us to the local school principal." A picture of a wild boar complete with tusks and flat nose flashed on the screen. The class roared uncontrollably.

Click.

Mrs. Hobson was now confused. She pushed th button and changed pictures.

"The colorful natives are proud of their new math teacher."

The class went into hysterics at the picture of a gray donkey.

Charlie suddenly felt a tight squeeze on his shoulder. The students had stopped their laughing. He turned his head and looked up—into the angry face of Mr. Rossini. Charlie's stomach suddenly knotted up and his face felt hot—he was sure it glowed in the darkened room.

"Well, Charlie Dean, you fooled Mrs. Hobson, but my ears are a little better than hers. Let's take a walk to the office—you too, Kerry. There's a matter of flying books that we need to discuss."

With their eyes pointed toward the floor, Charlie and Kerry silently followed the principal out the door.

"Your mother said I'd find you down here." Laura had been in Charlie's basement many times. It was packed with games, collections, books, stuffed animals and junk.

"Shhh," Charlie hissed. He held a camera in one hand while he arranged some items with the other. "You make more noise than a wrecking crew."

"Well, exc-u-u-se me! Your mother said Kerry and I may go to Salisbury with you. She wants to leave early to stop in Cambridge and see the Ludlow Diamond."

"Great! Sorry you can't stay longer right now." Charlie didn't bother to look up.

"By the way, what did your parents say after you got into trouble at school yesterday?"

"Mom was pretty upset—but I could handle that. Dad was another story. Mom told him just enough so that he came to me for an explanation. When I finished telling him, he gave me that real sad, disappointed look—I could hardly look him in the eyes. It's hard to do something wrong like that when your father loves you so much. It's worse than getting spanked."

"I can imagine. What did Mr. Rossini have you and Kerry do as punishment?"

"We had to wash all the blackboards in the school. Do you know how hard it is to wash twenty blackboards?"

"Frankly, I don't feel very sorry for you. I just hope

that you learned your lesson. What are you doing, anyway?"

"Never mind." He pivoted abruptly, hiding something on the table behind him. "I just happen to be very busy. Take a hike."

"I'm company. You need to treat me more nicely. What's behind you?"

Laura's hand darted out, but Charlie pushed it away. Quick as a cat her left hand shot around, hitting the black cloth. The dark material tumbled from the table, pulling a small green object with it.

"What's that?"

Charlie quickly scooped up the two items and clutched them in his hand.

"That's it, Laura. Now I'm going to have to get rough."

"Is that what I *think* it is?"

"I'm warning you." Charlie made a fist.

"A toy dragon. That's what it is."

"On three I'm throwing you out of here."

"A green toy dragon."

"One!"

"So that's what you meant by evidence."

"Two!"

"You're going to take a picture of a toy and try to pass it off as a Bay monster? What a banana brain."

"Wait'll you see how much it looks like the real thing."

"No matter, the picture's a lie."

"It's not what you think. I'm just going to take a picture to show people what the monster looked like, that's all."

"It's a lie."

"It's a *picture.*"

"A *lie.*"

"A *picture.*"

"Why don't you try reading the Bible sometime? You might be surprised at what it says."

"Cute, really cute."

"No one is ever going to believe this anyway. You can't make a toy look like a real monster."

"That's what you think. Just watch the master photographer operate."

Charlie quickly arranged the black cloth on the table, propping plenty of it behind the toy monster. Only the head and shoulders stuck out above the material.

"Hold this flashlight," he ordered.

"And become a partner in crime?"

"It's no crime, putty-head. It's just a picture."

"That doesn't even *look* like the Bay."

"Of course it doesn't. But it will, you just watch. Stand right here and aim the light at the monster's head."

"Hurry, before I change my mind."

"I'll set the shutter to one-sixtieth of a second."

"It won't look like the Bay."

"Stick with me, kid. Dad taught me how to use this camera. We'll take care of the Bay part later. Besides, what do girls know about cameras?"

"We know plenty," she protested.

Charlie snapped the picture.

"If no one touches this camera before I get out to the Bay, this photo will be a beaut."

"Mrs. Morgan!" Charlie called as he walked across the yard.

"Hello. You're Charlie, aren't you?"

"That's right."

"I just got back from Easton. I got some more bread in so I could feed the geese. I'm having a hard time getting their attention."

"Wild geese don't like to get too close to people. You probably won't have much luck."

"Oh, and I visited that magnificent museum in St. Michael's—the one with the crabs in the huge tank."

"The Maritime Museum is a favorite place around here for tourists. If you get near Salisbury, you'll want to stop at the college and see the Wildfowl Art Museum. It has some fantastic carved ducks."

"What a beautiful dog." Mrs. Morgan reached out and scratched the nape of Throckmorton's neck. The beagle turned his head away as if blushing.

"Don't worry, he won't bite you. Throckmorton is good at controlling his temper."

"Is he a good hunting dog?"

"The best. Not the fastest or the meanest, just the best."

"What do you hunt?" Mrs. Morgan ruffled the beagle's ears as he tried to bury his head against his chest.

"My dad takes us out to hunt cottontails. Throckmorton doesn't catch them but he keeps them running."

"Can you come inside a minute, Charlie?" She headed toward the door.

"Sure. Throckmorton can stay outside." He followed the lady into the house.

"If everyone hunts rabbits, they'll become extinct someday," she thought out loud.

"Far from it. The number of rabbits in the Bay

area isn't dropping at all. In fact, if their population isn't kept down, they do a lot of damage to crops."

"Do you enjoy eating them?"

"They're terrific. Rabbit tastes a lot like chicken. My mom adds a little onion, lemon, a tiny bit of garlic and some pepper. It's great."

"Do you think I'm too old to try hunting?"

"Not at all. You'd really enjoy it. It's fun to watch old Throckmorton pick up the scent of a cottontail. He'll chase it past my dad as many times as he needs to."

"I don't imagine I'm really going to go hunting, but I think about it. That's the trouble with most grandmothers. They just sit around and dream. But I want to try new things while I'm still healthy enough."

"The season starts in November and runs through January. I'm sure my dad would take you along."

"Thanks, but I don't think I'll be here that long. I get itchy feet and have to move on. There's one thing I would like to try, though."

"What's that?"

"I'd like to ride one of those hot-air balloons—those big colorful things I see sailing over the Bay. I'm tempted to go down and talk to one of the gentlemen who fly them."

"Lady, you sure have spunk."

"That's not all I have. I also have plenty of candy in that dish, and you'd better not run off until you get some."

Chesapeake Charlie would have a difficult time picking a favorite place around the Bay. He loved to talk with the friendly watermen on Tilghman Island. He often visited them as they unloaded crabs on warm afternoons.

Charlie also enjoyed going to beautiful Assateague and watching the ponies feed on the salty cordgrass. The area is famous for its annual roundup of the nearly wild ponies.

Thomas Point is high on Charlie's list because of its old, wooden lighthouse. It is the only manned lighthouse on the Bay.

When Charlie thought of places to go and things to try, his mind would start to swim.

But no place on the Bay was more fascinating to the happy adventurer than a crowded little store owned by his friend Woody. "Woody's" is located on Collin's Landing. No larger than a house trailer, it is jammed with crab pots, a candy counter, canned goods, a black, potbellied stove and a sandwich counter. A small table sits in the middle of the floor holding a well-used checkerboard and a set of dominoes. In slack times watermen sit around the table, slurp coffee and swap stories.

Woody's 70 years and snow-white hair made him, in Charlie's eyes, an authority on practically everything.

Charlie entered the little store. "Do you have C batteries? Pete wanted me to pick up some for his television game."

"I think I have half a dozen," answered Woody as he turned to a shelf. "How many do you need?"

"Six should do it."

Woody returned to the counter in a few seconds.

"Are people at your house talking about the Ludlow Diamond?" Woody asked.

"A little bit. A Maryland diamond is sort of unusual."

"No doubt about it. Another one was found across the Bay in Virginia, but that was many years ago. You just about have to have mountains to find diamonds."

"Dad said if we go through Cambridge, we might stop and see it."

"Some people think diamonds washed across the ocean floor over the centuries. There might be far more diamonds in Maryland than we imagine."

"I suppose a lot of people dream of finding diamonds and getting rich quick," Charlie said as he slipped the batteries in his jacket pocket.

"You wouldn't have to go far from here to get rich quick—not from diamonds, though. Just a mile or two beyond Easton, $50,000 worth of gold coins are supposedly buried. They were hidden during the Revolution somewhere around the Old Friends' Meeting House."

"There's more history around the Bay than a guy can keep up with, Woody." Charlie pointed through the glass case. "How about one of those Marathon bars?"

"Why in the world were you so insistent on going crabbing this evening?" Laura crouched down into her jacket like a turtle retreating into its shell.

"I know you don't like to miss a good catch," Charlie replied, rowing with strong determination.

"It's so cold already. Don't tell me you brought those goofy bull's lips again."

"Look behind you."

"Don't scare me like that," barked Laura. "I don't want to see that monster again."

"No, dummy, it's a skipjack."

A large boat sliced through the water with two white sails billowing in the wind. A full forty feet long, the craft sliced through the bouncing white caps, listing slightly to one side.

"What I wouldn't give to own one of those. There are less than thirty of them on the entire Bay," Charlie explained. "Someday they'll all be gone."

Skipjacks use winches to dredge oysters from the Bay. Metal baskets are dropped overboard and allowed to drag the bottom. When the baskets seem full, the workmen turn on the winch machine which pulls up the heavy catch. It is hard work but has an interesting history stretching back even before the Civil War.

"This looks like a good spot." Charlie pulled his oars in and laid them on the boat floor. Laura had tied pieces of chicken to strings and dumped them over the side. Instead of doing the same, Charlie reached for a box wrapped tightly in a plastic dry-cleaning bag.

"What have you got there?"

"It's my dad's camera. If I get it wet he'll probably sell me for crab bait."

"You aren't. . . !" Laura gasped.

"I am," Charlie retorted.

"You are dumber than I thought. You can't make a phoney picture."

"It isn't a phoney." Charlie freed the camera from its box.

"It's a lie, Charlie."

"Don't start that again. It's more like a practical joke."

"You're going to tell people the photo is a phoney, then?"

"Well, maybe not right away—but later."

"You really don't understand the difference between a joke and a lie, do you, Charlie?"

"Look, if I was going to hire a conscience, it wouldn't be you."

"When you and I kid each other it's fun. That's a joke. But if you seriously fool someone, that's got to be a lie. I think you're taking this one too far."

"Well, I don't think so. Now bug off; this is tricky."

"The devil is the father of lies you know. I'm sure you remember that verse from Sunday school."

"Shhh. Your voice will wake up the monster. I've got to do this exactly right. I turn the crank until it is nice and tight. Now I push the bottom button to release the film so it won't turn. Holding those two I then cock the shutter. That's it. The camera is cocked and ready to shoot, but I didn't move the film—a double exposure! Pure genius, don't you think?"

"Really neat. Maybe you can teach that to your friends in *prison.*"

"Girls could never learn that. You're just jealous."

"And what do you plan to do with this counterfeit?"

"It's the evidence Mrs. Morgan wanted to see."

"And then will you tell her you used a double exposure?"

"I certainly don't plan to do anything dishonest."

"Sometimes you get carried away with your humor," Laura warned.

"Look, back off and don't say anything. I want to see how realistic the photograph looks. That's not asking much. Sometimes you act like I'm not a Christian."

"I know you're a Christian, but some of the things you do are strange."

"Do you want to see something odd?" Charlie was relieved to change the subject. "Look at what's floating on the water."

"It looks like a wet hub cap."

"It's a moon jellyfish. You don't see many of them. It must be a foot and a half across."

"Do they sting?"

"Only little bugs. They can't do much to people."

"Yuck. It looks gross."

"You're pretty lucky. Not many people get to see one of those juicy creatures."

Chapter Four

It was early in the morning when the Deans drove through Easton. Mr. Dean turned right on route 50 and headed the car south toward Cambridge to see the Ludlow Diamond.

Six passengers filled the car. Pete sat up front between his parents, while Charlie, Kerry, and Laura occupied the back seat.

"Who wants to play quiz?" Laura asked.

"Like what?" Kerry wondered.

"I start off with, say—presidents—and we can each take turns being the quizzer," she replied. "All right. Name four presidents who were assassinated."

"That's easy," Pete jumped in. "Uh—Kennedy, Lincoln, McKinley and Cleveland."

"Nah, not Cleveland," Charlie corrected him. "It was Harding."

"You're both wrong," Laura announced. "It was Kennedy, Lincoln, McKinley and Garfield."

"It's my turn," Charlie jumped in. "Name an island in the Bay that used to be here but has disappeared."

"You mean *totally*?" asked Kerry.

"Right. Completely zapped," added Charlie.

"Who would know that?" Pete said.

"Certainly not landlubbers like you," Charlie retorted.

"What is it?" Laura asked.

"Sharp Island. It used to lie right up here in the mouth of the Choptank and people farmed it," Charlie answered crisply. "The water is claiming a lot of landmarks."

"When I was a girl you could still see part of Sharp Island," Mrs. Dean commented. "But it's gone now."

"How about a Bible question?" Laura asked. "Who was the man fed by black ravens?"

"Elisha," Charlie blurted out.

"Almost," Laura said.

"Elijah," Kerry ventured.

"On the nose," Laura conceded.

"We're practically in Cambridge," Mr. Dean announced.

The car rumbled over the Choptank River bridge, which lay directly at the threshold of Cambridge. Mr. Dean parked the car downtown.

"We can't stay long," Mr. Dean cautioned, "so let's go directly to the store and see the diamond. Your mother wants to pick up some things afterward. We'll have to leave as soon as she's finished."

A large sign filled one window of the store. It announced, "The Ludlow Diamond." The group filed inside and found the display in the center of the main floor. A blue-uniformed security guard stood next to the walnut stand.

"It's not in a very big case," Kerry whispered loudly.

"It's so beautiful! I love the tiny pedestal," Mrs. Dean responded.

"It's bigger than I thought," Laura said. "The lights really make it sparkle."

"Look at the card next to it," Kerry observed. "It says four things make the Ludlow Diamond valuable. All four start with 'C': carat weight, cut, clarity, and color. 'The Ludlow Diamond is colorless and almost flawless,' it says."

"It weighs six carats. Why do they call the weight 'carats'?" Charlie asked his father.

"I've heard that the word comes from an African fruit that looks like a bean—the Kurara. People used to compare a diamond's weight with a Kurara."

"That sounds like an odd way to check weight," Charlie concluded.

"But if you're discussing gold, karat is spelled with a 'K' and it doesn't mean weight but purity," Mr. Dean explained.

"How do you know all that?" Kerry asked.

"Because years ago I bought a diamond engagement ring for your mother and it was mounted on a gold band."

"Did it cost $50,000?" Charlie wondered.

Mr. Dean laughed. "Hardly—but don't tell her." He winked.

"That's what I'll tell my husband to get me." Laura held out her left hand, pretending to admire a ring on her finger. "I want the Ludlow Diamond, darling, or you can forget it."

"Any guy that would marry you would give you a ring with a whistle on it," Charlie snapped.

"Personally, I'm glad I don't have the ring," Mrs. Dean said.

"Why?" Charlie asked.

"Who wants to go through life with a security guard at one's side?"

"I think I'll start looking for diamonds when we get back home," Charlie declared. "I'll bet there are plenty of diamonds in Maryland."

With their curiosities satisfied, they left the store and split up in three directions. Mr. and Mrs. Dean set out for one store, while Kerry and Pete wandered through the shopping area.

"Let's get a Coke," Laura suggested to Charlie.

"Why not?" he replied as they walked across the street toward a pizza parlor.

They sat in a back booth and each ordered a soft drink.

"I read this morning that the Bay bridge is practically falling apart," Charlie began.

"Are you sure it's falling apart?" Laura frowned.

"Well, not really falling apart, but there are large cracks in that monster."

"Like how big? Oops! My contact lens fell out." Laura picked up her lens on her index finger as their drinks were delivered. "I'll never get used to these."

"Would you believe some cracks are four feet long?"

"And the whole thing is about to crumble?" Laura placed the lens on her tongue to moisten it.

"I didn't say that, but I do know that engineers can't find any way to stop the cracking."

She retrieved the lens so she could talk. "Do you worry about the bridge a lot?"

"No. It's just that water gets into the cracks and freezes and the cracks expand—that's all. Say, I've heard it's not very safe to moisten a contact on your tongue."

"Big deal." She placed the lens back on her tongue.

"Look," Charlie's hand hit his soda glass as he pointed toward Laura. Soda spilled across the table. Laura began giggling at Charlie's accident. Suddenly a look of despair flashed across her face.

"I swallowed it! I swallowed it!"

"You swallowed what?"

"My contact—it's gone." She looked pale as she spoke. "I can feel it lodged in my throat."

"Don't swallow anymore. Can you cough it up?"

Laura ran to the restroom. Inside she plugged the sink and began to cough into it. After several tries the tiny glass disc tumbled up into her mouth.

Sighing with relief, Laura washed her lens and inserted it in her eye. When she returned to the booth, Charlie was standing and making fun of her.

"Only a girl would do something dumb like that."

Her face turned red with embarrassment.

"You're lucky doctors didn't have to put long pliers down your throat and pull it up." Charlie stifled his laughter and turned to walk away. Laura grabbed the back pocket of Charlie's jeans with her left hand. In the same motion she took her glass and poured ice into the open pocket.

"Hey!" Charlie yelled.

"Laugh about that, Mr. Ice Bucket."

Laura grinned from ear to ear as she walked up to pay for her soda. Charlie mumbled to himself as he tried to pull pieces of ice out of his freezing pocket.

When Charlie and Laura sauntered out of the restaurant, they were both fuming. Pete and Kerry were coming toward them.

"What's bugging you guys?" Pete asked.

"As usual Laura has no sense of humor," Charlie snapped.

"You won't believe what we saw," Pete said.

"You remember that lady at the cottage—Mrs. Morgan?" Kerry asked.

"Is she shopping here?" Laura asked.

"She was in the candy store and did something strange," said Kerry. "When the saleslady wasn't looking, Mrs. Morgan opened a package of chocolate-covered marshmallows. Then she picked out a piece and pushed something shiny into it. I couldn't tell what it was. She put it back in the box and went to the cashier's counter."

"Then she called the saleslady," Pete added, "and tried to buy the package."

"The saleslady," Kerry continued, "saw the opened end and offered to get her another package—no way. Mrs. Morgan insisted on the package she had picked up."

"Isn't that weird?" Pete asked. "What do you figure she put into it?"

"Maybe your vision is playing tricks," Charlie speculated. "You sound as if *you* swallowed your contact."

Charlie immediately dashed down the sidewalk to get away from Laura. Angrily she put her hands on her hips and glared.

"What did he mean by that?" Kerry asked.

"Never mind. Why don't you ask him why the seat of his pants is wet."

The eastern shore of Maryland is flat, open, beautiful country. The six riders looked out the car windows on the neatly groomed farmsteads, old churches and thick groves of trees. Frequently restaurant signs advertised specials on hot, steamed crabs and oyster sandwiches. An occasional large billboard would invite travelers to an exciting vacation in Ocean City. Soon they were in Salisbury.

Mr. and Mrs. Dean wanted to visit some old friends near North Division Street so the four youths asked to be left off at the zoo.

"I'll show you some fantastic animals," Charlie said in his best "follow the guide" voice. "They have a couple of bears that you won't believe. Over there are wild Chincoteague ponies," Charlie proudly pointed out. "Just like the ones we saw at the roundup."

Laura watched the birds paddling freely on the Wicomico River. Kerry leisurely picked up a piece of old clothesline off the ground. They were doing nothing—four young people killing time together.

"Look at that grocery sack," Charlie said softly. "With that sack and your rope we could have some fun. Let's grab Pete."

No sooner had the words escaped Charlie's mouth than both boys dashed for the unsuspecting Pete. They wrestled him to the ground and began to tie his hands behind him.

"Grab that bag," Charlie called to Laura. Without a word she brought it to the attackers.

"Stand up," Kerry demanded.

Good-naturedly, Pete struggled to his feet. Half smiling and half aggravated, he snarled at his captors.

"When I get loose you three are going into the river."

"Enough talk." Charlie pulled the bag over Pete's head. "Lead him to the slide," he ordered with a deep voice.

With hands tied firmly behind him and a bag covering his head, Pete was led to the slide. Carefully he marched up the metal steps. After Pete sat down, Charlie gave his brother a hefty shove down the slide into the waiting arms of Kerry and Laura.

They kept this sport up for some time. Pete was sent down head first, feet first, lying on his back and then on his stomach.

"Guilty of treason on the high seas," Kerry announced as he took his turn sending Pete down. "Feed him to the sharks."

"Oh, oh. I wonder what they want." Charlie nodded toward two policemen walking in his direction. Pete came hurling into Laura's and Charlie's arms. Kerry thought he had best stay on top of the slide.

"What are you kids doing?" the first officer asked.

"Nothing, just having fun," Laura answered.

"From your friend's screams we're not sure if he *is* having fun," said the second policeman.

"Sure he is," Charlie assured. "He's my brother."

The first officer reached over and yanked the bag off Pete's head.

"Are you enjoying this?" the policeman asked.

"No, sir," Pete answered with his most pitiful look. "I'm sure glad you came along."

Both officers stiffened with concern.

"Oh, come on, Pete," Charlie protested.

"Do you know these people?" the second officer asked.

"I've never met them before," Pete lied. "They jumped me over by the bear pit. I hope you'll arrest them." Pete managed to control his frown and create a quiver in his voice.

"Hey, you, come down here," the first officer

yelled to Kerry. "Maybe we'd better go downtown and talk about this."

"You little wimp," Charlie growled at Pete. "Wait'll we get you."

"That's enough," cautioned the second officer. "I think you've made too many threats."

"We were just horsing around," Laura argued.

"The squad car is over this way," the first officer explained as he untied Pete.

"I don't believe this!" Charlie threw his hands up in the air.

"Wait'll my mother finds out," Kerry groaned.

"Where are you kids from?" the first policeman asked.

"Around St. Michael's," said Charlie. "My name's Charlie Dean. Look in his wallet and see if his lunch ticket doesn't say Pete Dean. It'll also say St. Michael's Elementary School."

"No need to," Pete said sheepishly. "I'm his brother."

"You are?" the second officer growled.

"I just wanted to get even with these guys for tying me up."

"Do you think this is a big game?" the first officer barked.

"Well, I was just kidding," Pete protested, hanging his head.

"You were lying," the officer continued. "You almost got your friends in big trouble. Hasn't anyone ever explained the difference between kidding and lying? We ought to run you all in to teach you a lesson."

The Dean car turned onto Pemberton Drive and

headed toward Anderson Lake. A weeping willow stretched its long limbs above the road.

"So Pete's a comedian," Charlie mumbled softly in the back seat.

"He loves to make big jokes at the wrong time," added Kerry.

Pete sat silently between his parents. A grin crossed his face, but he refused to look back or speak.

"This is where Charlie and Pete's mother grew up," explained Mr. Dean. "She still loves the farm."

"What kind of farm was it?" asked Kerry.

"A truck farm," Mrs. Dean replied. "We grew sweet potatoes, cucumbers, watermelons, beans, and other things. Then we would haul them to the produce auction in our truck."

"All the watermelon you could eat?" Laura licked her lips. She pointed to some old buildings on her right. "What was this?"

"A farmer used to raise turkeys and process them there."

"That would be a good place to leave Pete," Charlie grumbled. "He's a turkey."

Chapter Five

"I can't believe it!" Charlie paced the floor excitedly. "I can't believe it!"

"Well, you'd better calm down and eat your breakfast before you get left," Mrs. Dean warned. She had seldom seen Charlie so nervous.

"A skipjack, Mom; I'm going sailing on a skipjack! Dad said he's never been on a skipjack—and there are only a few left on the Bay."

Beep—beep.

"That's my ride!" Charlie jumped up.

"You didn't eat anything." Mrs. Dean handed a large lunch bag to Charlie as he pulled on an old, warm jacket.

"I'll pull my boots on in the car."

"Don't forget your rubber gloves."

"Everything's under control," Charlie insisted. "See you tonight."

Charlie grabbed the doorknob and made his exit.

Bang—bang—bang. Silence. The door slowly reopened. A very embarrassed Charlie had climbed back up the basement stairs.

"I took the wrong turn," he mumbled.

Mrs. Dean covered her mouth to muffle a laugh as Charlie rushed out the back door.

Charlie joined Laura and Kerry in the back seat of

an old station wagon. Two watermen sat up front.

"This is great of you to take us along Ned," Charlie said once he was settled.

The driver replied, "I try to get all the members of my Sunday school class on the skipjack each year."

Ned Andrews had sailed the Bay dredging oysters for the past twenty years. During most of those years he had taught the Junior High class at church. Young people enjoyed Ned Andrews.

It was hard to see the skipjack in the early morning darkness. More than forty feet of old, well-kept lumber marked the length of the craft. Charlie could barely make out the name, 'Free Spirit,' lettered on its side. Eagerly the group jumped on board.

Charlie, Kerry and Laura tried to stay out of the way. Six crew members worked feverishly to push off.

"We'll motor out into the Bay and hope there's enough wind to use our sails," Ned explained. "She sails pretty well for her age; she'll be 85 this year. But don't let that worry you. 'Free Spirit' is as good as new."

The skipjack had no motor of its own. A yawl, or pushboat, pushing against the stern, furnished power until it could sail alone.

The three adventurers stood on the foredeck and watched the busy crew. Charlie breathed deeply as a gentle breeze swept across the craft.

"I love that smell."

"It sure beats writing school papers," Laura observed.

"Do you think the men will let us help?" Kerry asked.

"Sure, once they start dredging," Charlie replied. "They'll need plenty of help to cull oysters."

"What does 'cull' mean?" Kerry wondered.

"It means to separate," Laura said.

"You divide the usable oysters from the bad ones. The ones you throw away are the culls," Charlie said.

The trio strolled curiously around the deck. Their excitement rose when Ned called, "Haul 'em up!" Sails began to unfurl as they were hoisted into position. "Pull out the jib," came another cry.

The three riders could smell sausage and eggs frying in the galley below. They wished they could hurry down the steps and invite themselves to breakfast—especially Charlie.

"We'll be dredging soon," Ned announced as he held a cup of steaming coffee to his mouth. "We'll pull up the yawl next and run on our sails."

"How long have you owned this rig?" Kerry asked.

"Always," Ned replied. "My father sailed her before me and his father before him. All of us have been fools." He grinned.

"It feels like a great life," Laura observed.

"Wouldn't trade it for anything," Ned answered. "Not much money, but it's nice to work for myself. My father had tough times, though. He had to carry guns in his day. Tongers and dredgers didn't always like each other. The old Oyster Navy even had a machine gun mounted on its cruiser. We all get along pretty well now. There aren't enough dredgers left to bother anybody."

"I'd never guess it used to be dangerous to be a waterman," Kerry said.

"Not as dangerous as being on land," Ned continued. "Did you hear the news this morning?"

"What?" asked Charlie.

"Somebody stole that diamond in Cambridge."

"The Ludlow Diamond?" Laura responded.

"The radio announcer said they don't know how it happened," Ned continued. "Yesterday someone noticed the diamond was a slightly different color. Evidently, someone replaced it with a phoney. I've got to grab that mainsail."

Kerry began, "It sounds to me like—"

"Don't say it," Charlie interrupted. "Little old Mrs. Morgan wouldn't do something like that. You let your imagination run wild."

"All I know—" Kerry attempted.

"You don't really know," Laura warned.

"Then what did she hide in the marshmallows?" Kerry blurted out.

"There's no telling what you and Pete saw," Charlie declared.

"Charlie," Ned called, "you want to take the helm for a minute?"

Charlie rushed toward Ned. He grabbed the wheel with both hands and looked out over the ship's bow.

"Keep it steady. We're near some oyster beds so I need to get the dredges ready," Ned explained.

"Look at that gorgeous bowsprit," Charlie told Laura as she joined him. He pointed toward the long, wooden pole that stuck out from the bow like a skinny, up-turned nose. "That gives a skipjack personality."

Laura pulled up her jacket against her chin to fight the cold breeze.

Charlie loved to watch the mainsail and jib arch tightly in the wind. The vessel sliced smoothly through the small, bobbing waves.

Two crew members slowly pushed a large steel basket over the port side. It was attached firmly to a long, tough cable. A second dredge basket followed.

"We will let them drag until we feel the baskets getting heavy with oysters," Ned explained. "Then we'll hoist them up and cull them. You three can help with that."

"How does he know when the basket is full?" Laura wondered.

"I think that's why his hand is on the cable," Charlie speculated. "I'll bet when the cable feels real tight Ned will pull it up."

"It's about ready." Ned's smile was friendly and relaxed. The three youths couldn't help but feel that he really enjoyed his work.

"Anything that isn't an oyster," he explained, "we'll push to the side and then dump overboard. It's dirty work but you'll enjoy it."

Charlie, Laura, and Kerry nervously pulled at their boot tops and adjusted their rubber gloves. Like competition skiers they readied themselves for the starting gun.

"Feels good to me!" Ned yelled. His hand hit a lever and the winch began to pull at the dark cables. Huge barrel spools started turning, wrapping the metal ropes around themselves.

When the basket reached the side of the skipjack, two crewmen grabbed it. They wrestled it onto the deck and dumped out sixty pounds of mud, shells, oysters and debris.

Experienced hands flew into the pile, separating prize from junk. Several crabs squirmed their way out of the mess only to be quickly captured.

"Keep an eye open for dinner," one burly crewman sang out as he flipped a crab into a bucket.

Laura tossed two soda cans and a beer bottle over to the side. Kerry dug into the mud to pull out a couple of good-sized oysters. Charlie's hands moved rapidly, tossing away empty shells and tumbling full oysters into the proper baskets.

As these workers were busy culling, two others lifted the dredge and sent it splashing into the water for another haul.

"Good job," Ned announced. "If it keeps up this well, we're going to have a good day."

"Here." The burly crewman handed a wide scoop shovel to Kerry. "Might as well send the waste back into the Bay."

Ned hit the second winch, and another dredge began to creak its way up onto the skipjack. Kerry had barely cleared the deck when the second load came crashing down. Arms and hands raced into action, sorting out the sticky catch.

Charlie, Laura, and Kerry pitched in enthusiastically. It was hard work but the thrill of being outdoors with fresh air brushing across their faces made the day fun.

At noon the crew took a break, shut off the winch engines, and washed up to eat. One of the watermen was an excellent cook. He kept meals frying, broiling, and steaming, and a coffeepot percolating.

"It's been a good morning," Ned told Charlie. "We already have nearly 100 bushels. We'll probably pull in our limit today."

"You have a limit?" asked Charlie.

"Sure thing. One hundred and fifty bushels. The

government doesn't want us to hurt the stock in the Bay. Like most things, if you don't take care of it, you'll be sorry later."

"Can't you just cheat and catch a few more?" said Kerry.

"I suppose you could, but I don't think there is much cheating. For one thing, the Marine Police are on the lookout for any watermen who break the law. But more important, most watermen are law-abiding, honest citizens. If they give their word, they keep their word. At least that's how I look at it."

"Otherwise it's lying, right?" Laura chimed in, giving Charlie a knowing glance.

"Of course," Ned agreed.

"And you couldn't tell the Marine Patrol you were just kidding," she continued.

"You wouldn't get away with it," Ned agreed.

"We all know that, Miss Policeman," Charlie said sarcastically.

"What's with the big lecture?" Kerry wondered.

"It's no lecture. It's just that a certain person doesn't know what a lie is." Laura bit loudly into an apple.

"Where do you sell the oysters?" Charlie said, changing the subject.

"When we're finished, we'll dock at the buyer's pier. He'll count the bushels as he hauls them off with a crane. He'll ship them quickly to New York, Baltimore, Washington, Ocean City, Philadelphia, Richmond, all around. Excuse me, I have to check the dredges."

"I'll have to buy a skipjack when I graduate," Charlie announced. "This is the life for me."

"Want some cookies?" Laura handed Charlie a small white bag.

"Thanks. Don't tell me you baked them."

"Maybe, maybe not." Laura walked away.

Charlie took one of the large chocolate cookies out of the tiny sack and bit into it. As he munched, Charlie noticed some writing on the bag: "Don't tell lies to each other; it was your old life with all its wickedness that did that sort of thing; now it is dead and gone" (Col. 3:9, TLB).

Half choking on his cookie Charlie jumped to his feet and yelled at the distant Laura.

"Just buzz off, girl!"

By evening Charlie was so tired that even his toes ached. The sun was beginning to set as Laura, Kerry, and Pete sat with Charlie on the backsteps of the Dean home.

"Remind me to never go on a skipjack again," Kerry moaned.

"How can you say that?" Charlie objected. "That was one of the greatest days of my life. Out on the Bay, free, making your own way—what more could a person want?"

"Maybe a new television game," Pete said dryly.

"What do you guys think about that diamond robbery?" Laura asked.

"Yeah, that did sound strange," Kerry said.

"Especially if you'd seen what we saw," Pete said. "I'll bet you that was the diamond Mrs. Morgan stuffed into the candy."

"Little old ladies don't steal diamonds—especially the Ludlow Diamond. That one took some *professional* criminals," Laura remarked.

"You're probably right," Charlie admitted. "But

don't be too sure. I once read a story about an old lady who was a murderer. No one suspected her, either."

"In books you can do anything," Pete insisted. "I read a comic book about a chicken that was trained to hypnotize people and pick their wallets. Its owner paid it off in sugared corn."

"Maybe we should get to know Mrs. Morgan better. After all, what do we know about her?" Charlie asked.

"What do we know about anybody?" Laura observed. "It's dumb to run around playing detective."

"We won't be playing detective. We'll just keep our eyes open," Charlie explained. "Besides, forget that for now. Look what my cousin sent me from Nebraska."

Charlie drew a white letter-sized envelope from his jacket pocket. He held it gently as if it were a rare treasure.

"What in the world is that?" asked Kerry.

"Something special."

"It's time for me to go." Laura started to rise.

"It isn't something girls can handle."

Laura settled back down. "Girls can handle a lot more than boys."

"Except, of course, for *this.*" Charlie tapped the envelope gently against the palm of his right hand.

"All right! All right! I give in—what is it?"

"Promise you won't scream?"

"I won't scream," she muttered. "Now let's see it."

"In here are six rattlesnake eggs."

"I'm leaving," Laura replied in disbelief.

"Girls really should."

"All right, let me see the rattlesnake eggs. They're

probably pebbles—from your head."

"They've been in the envelope for some time, so handle them gently."

Charlie placed the mysterious envelope lightly onto Laura's hesitant fingers. She accepted with all the caution due a high explosive.

"Go ahead, look at them," Charlie urged.

Carefully Laura began to open the envelope.

Rattle-rattle-rattle!

"Aaah! Aaah!" Laura threw the envelope into the air and leaped off the steps.

The three boys doubled over with laughter, roaring loudly.

Laura bent over to see the envelope she had tossed into the air. Beside it lay the object that made the rattling noise.

"I ought to strangle you, Charlie. And the same goes for you, Daffy Duck, and your funny friend, Elmer Fudd. I'm leaving."

"Wait. To prove we're friends, I'll show you how to make a rattlesnake.

"First you take a hairpin and bend the ends out to look kind of like a wide fork.

"Then you take a rubber band and string it through a button.

"Loop the ends of the rubber band on the ends of the hairpin. Then you wind the button around until it's tight. You then place the 'rattlesnake eggs' carefully into the envelope.

"If you don't touch it the button will stay still. However, if someone starts to open the envelope, the button will whirl around and make a noise like a rattlesnake.

"You can just call it genius." Charlie said with a grin. "Take it to school and try it on Mrs. Warren in Biology class."

Chapter Six

"Mrs. Morgan, Mrs. Morgan!" Charlie called as he knocked on the cottage door.

"I was hoping you'd come back soon, Charlie." She greeted cheerfully and invited him in. Throckmorton explored the yard.

"Well, I have something special for you," Charlie reported as he sat in an overstuffed chair. "You remember the Bay monster I mentioned seeing?"

"Of course. I've been wondering what it looks like."

"The evidence is finally back."

"Terrific—let me see."

"You're the first person to see this. It's an actual picture of the Bay monster."

Charlie pulled a 4" by 5" color photo from his shirt pocket and handed it to the eager lady.

"My goodness! It really is a monster! How did you manage to take this picture?"

"I was lucky. I just happened to have my camera with me when Laura and I went crabbing."

"You're an excellent photographer, especially considering you had to move quickly. The monster is centered and its green color is so sharp. What do you plan to do with the picture?"

"I'm thinking about showing it to the Coast Guard

or police. The problem is, I don't think they'll believe me."

"They'll believe *this* photo. Will you let me keep it for a couple of days? I'll show it to a few people and see what they say."

"Oh, I don't think so." Charlie reached for the photograph.

"Don't worry, I won't tell anyone who took it. It might help if I got some advice as to where you should take it."

"Well—I don't know."

Mrs. Morgan pulled open the drawer of the end table and dropped the photo in. In that short moment Charlie's startled eyes saw a silver, pearl-handled revolver resting in the drawer. His face froze in amazement.

"Don't give it another thought," she assured Charlie as she closed the drawer. "It's safe in my hands and I won't tell whom it belongs to. Here, have a candy kiss—take a couple." Mrs. Morgan pointed to the table.

Charlie's hand moved stiffly to take some chocolate. His mind was still fixed on the weapon.

"Uh, thank you," he mumbled.

"How was your trip on the skipjack?"

"It was fine, really great." Charlie spoke mechanically. His brain was trying to analyze what was happening.

"Did you dredge many oysters?"

"Yeah—yeah, plenty." Charlie began eating his candy when his eyes spotted another candy dish. it was a green bowl perched high on the old piano top. The bowl was filled with what looked like chocolate-covered marshmallows.

"We brought in 150 bushels. That's the legal limit." How could he get to those marshmallows without causing too much attention?

"Please excuse me a moment, Charlie. I have to pull some rolls out of the oven." Mrs. Morgan stepped through the door and into the kitchen.

Charlie checked to see if she was out of sight. His hand swooped to the bowl on the piano and grabbed several chocolate-covered marshmallows. He hurriedly jammed them into the pocket of his jeans.

Mrs. Morgan called from the kitchen, "Do you think your friend would take me on his skipjack sometime? I think I really would enjoy that."

"Why sure. That is, I imagine. That depends on how long you plan to stay here."

"Probably two more weeks." She walked back into the room.

"Well, I'll see what I can do. I have to run now," Charlie said nervously, "but I'll be back."

"Anytime. And bring your friends along."

All that night and the next day Charlie had trouble concentrating. School dragged on. Visions of a pearl-handled revolver, chocolate marshmallows, and the glittering Ludlow Diamond kept dancing through his mind.

"Only Laura, Pete, and you can know about this," Charlie cautioned as he slipped his arms through the straps of his backpack.

"Still, it's hard to believe," Kerry answered. He bent over to retie one of his sneakers. "Are you *sure* you saw a pistol?"

"Shhh! Absolutely. What I'm not sure of is how

long she'll stay before she skips town. She said she'd leave in about two weeks, but I don't believe it."

"Why don't we just go to the police and let them settle it?"

"Great. I'm going to walk into the police station and say that Mrs. Morgan from Pittsburgh has the Ludlow Diamond stuffed in a chocolate marshmallow. They'll laugh me out of the place."

"You're probably right," Kerry said, walking toward the door. "But why doesn't she just skip town right away?"

"Maybe she's afraid to raise suspicion. If she hangs around and plays it cool, no one is going to suspect a kind lady like her."

"I s'pose our biggest problem right now is getting our hands on those chocolate-covered marshmallows."

"Without making Mrs. Morgan suspicious."

"You took the photo to her, didn't you?" Laura snarled at Charlie.

"You're jealous, lady. You wish you had thought of it." Charlie tied a balloon around a crab's claw.

"Will you put that crab down and listen to me. Besides, Kerry has already done this dumb balloon trick."

"Mrs. Morgan was so impressed with the photo she asked to keep it. And Kerry didn't do what I am about to do." Charlie tied a second balloon to the bewildered creature.

"And when do you plan to tell her the truth? Or don't you?"

"In good time, my dear." Charlie attached his

third helium-filled balloon. "Now you'll have to admit I'm a master genius."

Charlie licked his index finger and raised it to check the wind direction. "It's perfect." He released the crab and allowed the balloons to carry it across the yard.

"Now be quiet. I have to do this at the right time."

Charlie picked up his BB rifle and aimed it carefully. "When it floats across that turned-overed boat, I'll zap the balloons," he said calmly. "It has to land just on the other side. Steady . . . steady. . . .

"Now."

Pop. The first balloon exploded.

Pop. The second balloon followed.

Pop. The crab dropped behind the boat.

Woof! Woof! Woof!

Throckmorton barked, howled and yelped as he struggled to his feet. Running full force, the beagle stumbled over himself trying to escape the attacker from outer space.

Stopping behind a tree, the dazed dog peered around to see if he was being followed. Throckmorton watched intently as the frightened crab raced sideways toward water and freedom.

"You really can be mean," Laura said with a scowl.

"Come here, Throckmorton." The bashful beagle trotted toward his master. "He knows I was only kidding."

Charlie patted the back of his neck and ruffled his long ears. Throckmorton snuggled against Charlie's leg. They were old friends and a couple of tricks couldn't disturb the affection they had for each other.

"You guys want to come along?" Kerry's familiar voice echoed across the yard. "I'm going down to the point to look for horseshoe crab shells."

"What for?" asked Laura.

"I'm decorating the inside of my clubhouse with them. Come on, you can help me."

Horseshoe crab shells are as large as hub caps. Their empty shells are marine green and are plentiful around the Bay.

Kerry, Laura, Charlie, and Throckmorton decided to walk the mile down the road to the point. It was a favorite place to explore and watch a wide variety of boats and ships glide across the Bay.

"What do you think this is from?" asked Kerry as he picked up a large, weathered block of wood.

"It certainly looks old," Laura agreed.

"We oughta keep it," Charlie ventured. "It's probably off an old ship—maybe a hundred years old or more. Woody could tell us something about it." He kicked at an old radiator hose lying on the sand.

Kerry parked the rotted board against a tree and rejoined the hunt. One of the most interesting places on the point to search was a large pile of rocks and boulders. Many surprises became caught in this area. They had found everything from sea nettles to ship parts lodged among the rocks.

The water made walking tricky. As the tide came in in the evening the boulders would be practically covered—and slippery.

"Look what's floating over here," Kerry called. His legs stretched widely as he reached for an old black boot. As his weight shifted on the edge of the rock the huge stone moved.

"Hey!" Kerry yelled as the rock dropped beneath the water taking Kerry with it. Kerry collapsed into a hole with the rock tumbling along side.

"Hey, help!" he yelled again.

Charlie and Laura hurried over laughing as they hopped from rock to rock.

"You're a real klutz," Charlie teased. He began to laugh at the comical sight. Kerry's chin was just above the water line.

"Are you okay?" Laura asked.

"I think so. My leg hurts. Here, take my hands."

Charlie and Laura each grabbed an arm. They pulled, but Kerry didn't move. They strained harder. He didn't budge.

"Stop clowning," Charlie complained. "We won't help if you're going to play games."

"I don't know what's wrong."

"What do you mean?" Laura asked.

"The boulder is on my leg and it won't move."

"Is your leg all right?" Charlie became concerned.

"I'm not sure. It hurts quite a bit."

"I don't think he's kidding," Laura said.

"Pull his arm, Laura. I'll take the other one." Worry flooded Charlie's face. They both tugged and strained but Kerry didn't move.

"You *are* in a fix," Charlie conceded. "And you had to find a drop-off. All those shallow places and you find deep water."

"Someone will have to go under and move that boulder," Laura explained.

"All right, old buddy." He tapped Kerry on the head. "I'm going down." He pulled off his shoes and threw them on the beach.

Kerry wasn't smiling. This was serious.

Charlie took a deep breath and ducked under the surface. Kerry filled up most of the opening between the rocks. There was no way to turn around so Charlie bent his knees and reached for the rock.

He fingered the outline of the boulder for a good spot to grab, then to push. There was no movement. He pulled. No movement. Charlie surfaced for air.

"I'll try it the other way." He dove head first. Holding on to Kerry's body, Charlie made his way to the bottom. He wrestled with the rock but couldn't cause it to shift. Charlie wiggled back to the top, feet first.

The water had risen slightly above Kerry's chin. Charlie knew what that meant but didn't want to say it.

"Laura, we can't both dive down there. You'd better go for help. The Burns' house is half a mile from here. Hurry!"

"Be right back." Laura ran across the beach toward the woods.

"The tide is rising, isn't it?" Kerry asked.

"I'll get that rock rolling."

Charlie dove again. The water was cold but this time he stayed longer. He tugged harder. When he surfaced, his chest was pumping painfully and he struggled for each breath. When he coughed the veins on his neck expanded against his red skin.

"It won't take long!" Charlie gasped. "Laura won't take long."

The water had closed in at Kerry's ears. He stretched to hold his mouth above the surface.

Charlie didn't want to show Kerry how concerned

he really was. He looked up and down the shoreline but saw no one who might help. A boat was passing but it was so far away it seemed little more than a dot. Charlie clenched his teeth and closed his eyes. Silently he prayed. "Lord, we're in *big* trouble. If Kerry doesn't get loose he's going to drown. Please, God—please send someone to help us!"

When Laura reached the Burns' house, she was puffing like a steam engine. She pounded on the front door but no one came. With all the strength she could muster, Laura cried, "Help! Help!" She pounded again. There was no answer.

Her mind whirled, trying to come up with a solution. Should she go back to Charlie and Kerry? What help could she be there? There was another house farther down the road. Laura sped off.

Running full speed she sped into the woods and crashed through the brush. Laura approached a fallen log and leaped to clear it. Her heel caught a vine. She stumbled and her head thudded against a tree as she fell. She rolled on the ground and stopped face down. Laura lay motionless.

Kerry stretched his neck as high as he could. The rising cold water was making his teeth chatter. Charlie had gone down a couple more times and was now exhausted.

"Where is she?" Charlie angrily smacked his hand on the rock.

Whenever Kerry relaxed his neck, the water covered his lips. Charlie's mind groped for an answer to the predicament. It was too late for him to go for help. As the sun set across the Bay, their problems seemed to grow worse.

Suddenly an idea hit Charlie. If it worked, they might be able to buy more time. He leaped across the rocks and dashed across the beach. He found the length of radiator hose and sped back to Kerry. He sloshed the black rubber tube in the water to rinse off the sand.

"It's not very clean, but it's all I could find." He handed it to Kerry. "Put this end in your mouth and breathe through it. Keep the other end above the water."

Kerry didn't say anything; his eyes were big with fear. He took the tube in his shaky hand and held it to his lips.

Charlie hurried toward the beach again.

"I'll try to find something to move that rock!" he yelled.

Charlie scoured around the rocks until he found a large tree limb.

"It's worth a try," he told Kerry as he returned.

Charlie dove toward Kerry's feet. He wedged the limb beneath the rock and strained against it. The added leverage caused the boulder to budge only slightly. After several tries Charlie returned to the top.

Charlie labored for air. He was startled to see how high the water had risen. Kerry's mouth was covered and the water was almost up to his nose. Charlie looked across the beach.

"Where is that girl?" he muttered.

Charlie dove under again. He grabbed the limb and pushed so hard he thought he would explode. It budged. He pushed again. The rock started to roll.

Charlie's lungs ached for air, but he worked harder. Push . . . roll. Push . . . roll. Each time it settled back into place. Push . . . roll. Push . . . roll. Push . . . the rock flopped over on its side, freeing Kerry's foot.

Kicking with all his strength, Charlie struggled to the top. Charlie gasped violently as he broke the surface. His face and mouth screamed for joy, but his lungs didn't have any air left to make a noise.

The boys hugged each other clumsily. Kerry was free!

Leaning on each other, they staggered across the rocks onto the shore. Kerry was in terrible pain as he dragged his foot behind him.

"I'm afraid it's broken," Kerry wheezed with tears in his eyes. The boys looked at each other, grabbed the other's shoulders, hugged and cried silently.

They didn't notice the pickup truck that pulled up behind them. Laura and some neighbors quickly climbed out.

Chapter Seven

"It's the police," Pete whispered, pointing to the car parked in front of Mrs. Morgan's house.

"Now I won't get my picture back," Charlie whined. "And Mrs. Morgan is probably going to jail for stealing that diamond."

"What picture?" Pete asked with a puzzled look.

"Forget I said it. I wonder how they caught her so quickly."

"The police are pretty shrewd."

"Maybe we'd better just go back home," Pete suggested.

"Wait a minute. I need to get that picture. Let's go on inside—it will give us a chance to see how the police work. Besides, if they take her belongings, my photo is gone forever."

The boys walked onto the porch and pounded on the door.

"What photo, Charlie?"

"Don't worry about it. I'll explain when you grow up."

"Mrs. Morgan! Mrs. Morgan!" they yelled.

They were surprised to see the white-haired lady answer the door. Two police officers stood behind her in the living room.

"We hate to bother you, Mrs. Morgan," Charlie said sheepishly.

"It's no bother at all; come right in."

"Are—are you sure we should?" Charlie stammered.

"Absolutely." Mrs. Morgan took Charlie's arm and guided him through the doorway. Pete followed stiffly.

"We were talking about you just this minute."

Charlie gulped.

"This is Officer Ambrose and—and Officer Hartford. You'll never guess what I did—you'll be so proud!"

"What's that?" Charlie asked weakly.

"I showed them your excellent photo." Turning to the officers, she continued, "This is the Charlie I told you about. His friends call him Chesapeake Charlie."

Charlie felt faint and pale. He had a sudden wish for wings, a trapdoor or vanishing cream—anything that would get him out of there.

"This is interesting," Officer Ambrose said, looking at the photo. "We don't usually make a big deal out of monster sightings. We hear about one every couple of years. However, an actual photograph is highly unusual."

"Oh?" Charlie squeaked.

"Now, correct us if we're wrong," Officer Hartford said. "You did take this picture, didn't you?"

"Uh, sure."

"And it was in the Bay?" Hartford continued.

"Yes, sir."

"Well, we aren't authorities on photography," Officer Ambrose added. "The best thing we can do is take it down to headquarters and show it to the chief. He might want to give it to the Coast Guard, the Marine Patrol, or he might want to talk to you."

"Sure, uh, why not?"

"We'd appreciate it if you would sign this." Officer Hartford handed Charlie a clipboard and a pen. "It simply says this photograph belongs to you. That way you'll get it back when we're finished with it."

Charlie's throat felt dry as he wrote his name. He worked hard to keep his hand from trembling.

"We're glad you dropped by, Charlie," Officer Ambrose said as the men started for the door. "It saved us the trouble of searching around Collin's Landing for you." He glanced again at the photo. "Boy, that monster is an ugly dude."

"You mean that's all you wanted?" asked Charlie.

"Why sure. Were you expecting something else?" Officer Hartford asked.

"You're not here for some other reason? I mean—I mean—anything else?" Charlie rolled his eyes toward Mrs. Morgan.

"Not to my knowledge." Hartford concluded, "Well, we'll probably be talking to you later." The door banged behind the officers.

"I hope you didn't mind my showing that to the police," said Mrs. Morgan after the officers left. "They seemed like such nice gentlemen."

"Oh, not at all. I'm glad you did."

Charlie was starting to feel more confident. At least three people had seen the picture and none of them suspected it was rigged. Fear began to leave and pride took its place.

"So the cops have the picture," Laura commented as she tied her skate lace.

"That's right, and they're going to show it to their boss. They seemed like real smart men." Charlie twirled an orange umbrella in his hands.

"Too smart to fall for this hoax, pinball brain? I bet you'll look great in a prison uniform. And Pete just stood there and let you lie?"

"What do you want from me? I didn't know anything about it."

"Don't you care if your brother goes to jail? I suppose you'll be glad to get rid of him."

"No one is going anywhere." Charlie assured. "They're probably going to name the monster after me: the Dean Bay Monster—no, the Charlie Dean Monster. I'll figure something out.

"Okay, you two, line up behind me. Now you have to do exactly as I tell you if this is going to work right."

"I hope this works better than some of your stupid schemes, Charlie Dean," said Laura.

Laura lined up behind Charlie and Pete followed her.

"Hold onto my belt and, Pete, you grab Laura's. We need to skate in unison at first—but not too fast."

"We're set," Laura answered.

"Okay. Left . . . right . . . left . . . right. . . ."

The trio skated smoothly along the asphalt bicycle trail. When they began to gain good speed, Charlie held his orange umbrella straight out. A steady tail wind caught the umbrella and began pushing them.

"Coast!" Charlie shouted, "Coast!"

Each member stood stiff-legged and let the breeze do the work. Cars passed them on the highway and the passengers stared at the sight.

The wind was strong enough so they kept rolling right out of Collin's Landing. As other children saw the human train, they also joined. Two young people with skates latched on behind Pete. Four or five on bicycles soon tagged along. The cyclists began sounding their horns and ringing bells.

It quickly became a small parade. Dogs and cats brought up the rear. Since the highway didn't have an intersection for a long distance, they traveled uninterrupted.

A policeman spotted the growing line, so he drove slowly past them and waved a friendly "hello." Then it dawned on the officer how he might help. Pushing on the accelerator, he hurried to the nearest intersection. When the wind-powered parade came to the corner, the smiling policeman stopped all traffic and allowed Charlie and his crew to sail through without difficulty.

Chesapeake Charlie felt like king of the Bay. His legs hardly tired as the wind pushed his parade down the highway.

"That's a good picture of your parade in the paper, Charlie," Mrs. Dean remarked as the family sat in the living room.

"I don't know how they got that," Charlie replied.

"Well, they had plenty of time," Mrs. Dean added. "You must have traveled half way across Maryland."

"And that orange umbrella was easy enough to spot," Pete commented, looking up from his computer football game.

"Say, how about trying a little quiz?" Mr. Dean

asked. He enjoyed playing games with his family. It gave them a chance to turn off the television and talk with each other.

"Sure," Charlie said. "What do you want us to do?"

Mr. Dean gave paper and a pencil to each of the boys and their mother.

"I'm going to read a list of commandments—I have twenty of them. For each one of the Ten Commandments, write down true. For the others, write false. It's that simple. Here goes:

"One, you will not irritate your brother.

"Two, you will not use God's name in vain.

"Three, you will keep the Sabbath.

"Four, you will not be late for supper.

"Five, you will not sing on Sunday.

"Six, you will honor your parents.

"Seven, you will not murder.

"Eight, you will not call people names.

"Nine, you will not commit adultery.

"Ten, you will not steal.

"Eleven, you will not tease teachers.

"Twelve, you will not lie."

Immediately Charlie pictured Laura chewing him out. He fought hard to shake her from his mind.

"Thirteen, you may not worship any other God.

"Fourteen, you will not have a messy room.

"Fifteen, you will not worship idols.

"Sixteen, you will do the dishes.

"Seventeen, you will not envy others.

"Eighteen, you will not play computer football after bedtime.

"Nineteen, you will not get angry.

"Twenty, you will get up early."

The Dean family laughed and teased as they wrote their answers down. They felt very close to each other when they did such things together.

"Here are the real commandments," Mr. Dean announced. "Two, three, six, seven, nine, ten, twelve, thirteen, fifteen and seventeen. How did you do?"

B-r-ring.

Charlie jumped up to answer the phone. He was surprised to hear Mrs. Morgan's voice.

"You'll never guess what Mrs. Morgan wanted," Charlie said when he re-entered the living room.

"She wants to go sky diving," Pete kidded.

"Worse than that. She's rented a hot-air balloon and wants Laura, Pete and me to go along."

"That sounds dangerous," Mrs. Dean observed.

"It really isn't," said Mr. Dean. "In fact, it's probably one of the safest rides on the Bay. It's expensive though—over $200 an hour. If Mrs. Morgan has that kind of money, it's all right with me."

Ballooning wasn't entirely new to the Dean family. In the two previous summers, they had attended the Great Chesapeake Bay Balloon Rally in Annapolis. But they were baffled that a lady of Mrs. Morgan's age and quiet life-style would want to try it. Ballooning was something Charlie had long dreamed of. Immediately he searched for books to see what he could learn about it.

How could she possibly be a diamond thief? Charlie thought. He and his friends had surely been mistaken about her. A pearl-handled pistol and a chocolate-covered marshmallow didn't make someone a crook. But inside him, he still had a strange feeling about Mrs. Morgan.

A hot-air balloon was one of the greatest sites on the Bay for Charlie. There were so few they were still a novelty and they caused a stir wherever they went. Balloons are able to fly in any season, but around the Bay they are more likely to be seen in the fall and spring.

"It's a perfect day for ballooning!" Al Langdon exclaimed as he gazed at the cool autumn morning. Al was an experienced pilot who obviously loved flying his craft.

"The crew will have her filled in a few minutes—then we can launch. If you guys want to help, just jump in anywhere."

Balloon material was stretched out across the ground for fifty feet in a straight line. Several people helped hold the throat open while air was forced in with a fan. The pilot then turned on the gas burners and hot air was blown into the billowing material.

"Look at those gorgeous colors!" Mrs. Morgan cried. The orange and yellow section puffed up like bread rising in the oven.

"It's filling fast!" Charlie shouted.

Crew members held onto lines to keep the balloon from blowing away as it filled. Pete helped with the crown line. Attached to the top of the balloon, it made the craft manageable under pressure.

"That basket isn't very big, is it?" Laura asked Pilot Langdon.

"Wicker baskets aren't, but this will hold the five of us."

"Where are the sandbags?" Charlie asked.

"Oh, you mean the ballasts? We don't need those with a burner. If we want to go up or down we simply turn the burner up or turn it down. That regulates the amount of hot air."

"How cold will it be up there?" Mrs. Morgan asked.

"About the same as down here. We'll go up only about 500 feet so the temperature should be the same."

"Does it carry liquid propane?" Charlie asked, showing off the knowledge he'd gained.

"That's right. How did you know?"

"I looked it up."

"The fuel tank is in the bottom of the wicker basket, but the heat comes out over our heads."

"Do we take parachutes along?" asked Laura.

"They aren't necessary. Balloons almost never have trouble; if there is a problem, the best escape is to lower the balloon. It's ready, let's hop in."

Mrs. Morgan, Charlie, Laura, Pete and Al Langdon clambered into the brown basket and prepared to lift off. The crew members stood back holding the lines, ready to let go at the pilot's command.

"Won't we need oxygen masks?" Pete asked.

"No, you dense. We aren't going that high," Charlie scolded.

"Let'er go!" the pilot yelled. His hands moved skillfully across the small set of controls. The flame leaped up sending more hot air into the yawning balloon. Smoothly the bulb-shaped yellow and orange balloon rose from the ground.

Charlie could feel his stomach swim as the craft

rose. He forced a faint smile so no one would know how uncomfortable he felt. The dizzy sensation didn't last long. In a few minutes all five were talking easily and enjoying their new adventure.

"What is this side rope for?" Mrs. Morgan asked.

"That one is tricky to handle," Pilot Langdon explained. "It's another reason why we don't need sandbags to control our altitude. If I need to go down, I can just turn off the heat valves and pull that rope. The rope opens a slit in the side of the balloon and allows hot air to escape. When you let go, it closes again. It's perfectly safe."

"Aren't you afraid of being hit by an airplane?" Laura asked.

"What a dumb question!" Charlie teased.

"Not really," the pilot corrected. "That's why most of us have such loud-colored balloons. If it was just a white balloon, a pilot might not see us and wreck us—and himself—in a hurry.

"The fields and the water look beautiful from up here!" Mrs. Morgan exclaimed.

"Right now we're about as high as the top of the Washington Monument. We have a good view without too much danger. Watch our altimeter; it'll tell you how high we are."

"I don't feel any wind," Laura said.

"Good observation. Our balloon is so light it moves *with* the wind. That makes it hard to feel the breeze since we're part of it."

"Wow, look at the Benson place!" Charlie yelled. "Man, it's a mansion! I didn't know there were so many buildings on the place. That must be Bensons' house. It's huge!"

"I feel like we're peeking in everyone's backyard," Mrs. Morgan said with a giggle.

"Could you take someone *across* the Bay?" Charlie asked.

"No problem. All we have to do is plan ahead. There's no place to land on the water, so we make sure conditions are perfect."

"You mean no storms?" Charlie asked.

"Certainly, we don't want a storm, but there are other factors. The wind has to be just right; it has to be strong enough and going in the right direction. If we ran out of wind, the trip could get exciting awfully fast."

"How high will these babies go?" Charlie asked.

"This one won't break any records, but some balloons have gone amazingly high. Twenty years ago two men took a balloon up to 113,000 feet. That's higher than most planes go."

"It's so quiet up here—almost peaceful," Mrs. Morgan said contentedly.

"Except for these burners there's no noise. And if you've been up as often as I have, you don't even notice them."

"Aaaugh!" Pete made a terrible sound as he whirled and leaned over the side.

"Here, give Pete a bag," Al Langdon ordered. "The people on the ground don't appreciate someone throwing up out of a balloon."

The bright balloon soared without a bump across the soft blue sky. Charlie stood tall in the wicker basket and breathed deeply of the clear, open air.

"Look at the geese." Charlie pointed at the V-shaped flock as it passed them. "What could be better than to be sailing by the Bay watching God's world under your feet? Man, this is freedom!"

Laura and Charlie were eating in the school cafeteria when Kerry hobbled in. He managed his one crutch well.

"How's the foot?" Laura asked.

"Better all the time," Kerry answered as he sat next to Charlie. "The sprain is pretty bad but the doctor said I'm lucky it wasn't broken." Kerry tossed his lunch bag on the table.

"Did you watch the Colts game?" Charlie asked.

"Yeah, what a cream. How can you lose to the Giants? You'd think the Colts were *trying* to lose!"

"Forget about the fuzzy football game," Laura interrupted. "We have more important problems. Charlie still thinks Mrs. Morgan is the diamond thief."

"Me too," Kerry agreed. "What do you think that marshmallow candy thing was about, anyway?"

"We're going to end up fooled on this one," Laura insisted. "Nice old ladies don't steal diamonds."

"Nice old ladies don't keep pearl-handled pistols in their houses, either," Charlie objected.

"Sure they do," Laura insisted. "Lots of ladies have guns to protect themselves."

"It would be easy enough to find out. All we have to do is get that dish of candy," Kerry suggested.

"That's easy to say," Charlie said. "Besides, we don't have much time. She might be packing to leave right now."

"It wouldn't be a big deal," Laura concluded.

"What's that?" asked Kerry.

"Getting that candy."

"How?" wondered Charlie.

"I was just thinking. Adults trust girls more than boys because we're nicer."

"Not that again," Kerry moaned.

"Well, it's true. But what would it prove? Even if the diamond was in the dish, she's probably moved it by now."

"And maybe not," Charlie added. "It's a perfect hiding place." He thought for a moment. "But it's too dangerous. I couldn't let you go."

"Couldn't let me go! Who do you think you are—my nursemaid? I can do what I want and I don't need permission from a square-eared boy."

"Square-eared?" Charlie growled.

"That's right."

Kerry was enjoying the argument, laughing at each exchange.

"I'll go over and solve this thing once and for all," Laura insisted.

"I won't let you," Charlie commanded.

"Oooh! Oooh!" Laura's face turned red with anger. She quickly scooped up a spoonful of vanilla pudding and aimed it at Charlie.

"Don't do it Laura—Laura!" he yelled.

Ploop! The pudding splattered against Charlie's shirt. Laura grabbed her lunch tray and marched off.

"Typical woman—can't control her temper," Charlie murmured as he looked at his soaked front. Kerry snickered loudly.

"Say. Where's my lunch bag?" Kerry finally asked. "Did Laura take my lunch?"

"No," Charlie answered angrily, "and you can thank me for hiding it for you."

Charlie stood to return his tray—Kerry saw his lunch. The bag was squashed flat on the seat where Charlie had been sitting.

Chapter Eight

Mrs. Morgan welcomed Laura into the living room. "I'm so glad you could come over. As you can see, I've been baking. I thought I'd invite you, Charlie, Kerry and Pete over for a little party."

"That would be fun." Laura forced a nervous smile.

"Are you on your way home from school?"

"I had gym today—that's why I have two bags." A red and white gym bag hung from her hand and a knapsack of books hung from one shoulder.

"Have a seat and I'll pour you a glass of soda pop."

Laura fidgeted on the edge of the chair. Her eyes wandered around the room. She saw a dish of candy kisses but no chocolate marshmallows.

"Here," Mrs. Morgan said as she handed Laura a glass of soda.

"I wanted to thank you again for that exciting balloon ride. It was much smoother than I thought it would be."

"It's fun to try new things, isn't it? Last year I went hang gliding—and at my age!"

"How much longer will you be able to stay?" Laura nervously fished for things to say.

"Just two more days. That's why I want to have

you kids over. Excuse me a minute."

Mrs. Morgan hurried back into the kitchen. Laura's eyes darted to the old piano and the green dish on top. That was it! Chocolate marshmallows. Quietly, Laura unzipped her gym bag. She started to stand up.

"The cookies are doing just fine." Mrs. Morgan hurried back into the room and startled Laura.

"Oh, uh, where will you be going from here?" she stammered.

"Probably back to Pittsburgh. But I have thought of stopping in Philadelphia. I have some good-looking nephews and nieces there. Have I ever shown you their picture?"

"I don't think so."

"Well, sit tight. It's in the bedroom."

As Mrs. Morgan left, Laura jumped to her feet. In three long steps she reached the piano. With one wide sweep Laura grabbed the green dish and dumped its contents into her bag. Briskly she returned to her chair.

"The picture is a bit dusty," Mrs. Morgan apologized, "but they are darling children."

Laura looked at the picture. "They're terrific," she said lamely. "I'm afraid I have to get going." Laura bent down for her bag. As she stood Laura found herself looking into the barrel of a pistol.

"Maybe you'll want to leave the marshmallows with me," Mrs. Morgan said dryly.

Laura wanted to reply, but her throat was suddenly tight. She could feel the color leave her face.

"Why did you want to complicate matters? A couple more days and I would have been gone. Now I have to change my plans. I also have to decide what to do with *you*."

"Don't worry about me. Here, take the marshmallows and I'll just go on home."

"That sounds easy to you, but I think you know too much. I'm too old to go to jail. No, I'll have to do something about you—you nosey brat."

"Charlie," Mr. Dean called to his son in the backyard. Charlie was reloading his fishing reel.

"Have you seen today's paper?" his father asked.

"Not yet," he replied without looking up. "Is there anything good in the sports?"

"No, but there's something quite amazing on the front page—a picture of a Bay monster."

Charlie's face dropped with shock.

"The paper says this picture belongs to Charlie Dean. What's this about?"

"Well, I—well, I . . . "

"You told me you saw a monster, but you didn't say anything about a picture."

"Well, I was going to explain it, but—"

"Is this your picture?"

"Well sure, but—"

"But what?"

"It's hard to explain, Dad."

"Look, Son, I don't know what's going on, but I don't like the looks of it. I think if my son had a picture like this, he would have told me about it."

"Everything's all right, Dad. Just give me a little time and I'll tell you all about it."

"I'll give you a little time—but I want the truth. If you really took the picture—"

"Oh, I took the picture."

"Then I want to know why you didn't tell us and I want to know how the newspaper got ahold of it. Your Aunt Wendy has already called to ask, and I know our friends will want to know. What am I supposed to tell them?"

"It's really simple, Dad. Just give me a little time."

Charlie rushed through the door of Woody's store, all out of breath.

"You look, upset, Charlie," Woody told him. "Why don't you drink a soda?"

"Thanks, Woody, but I'm afraid I've really messed up this time. Have you seen Laura?"

"Not this evening."

"I've looked everywhere. She isn't home and she's not with any of her friends."

Charlie took a big gulp of soda.

"Have you seen the newspaper?" Charlie asked when he finished swallowing.

"Well, I did for a few minutes. My copies sold out like gold nuggets."

"Nuts!"

"You really know how to become famous in a hurry."

"It isn't funny."

"Why not?"

"It looks like I have myself in big trouble."

"You mean about the picture?"

"Exactly."

Woody stared at Charlie for a moment.

"Hm-m. I don't know what your problem is, but

let me tell you about a problem I had. It might help you to solve yours.

"A salesman came by once and sold me a dozen plastic wind-up cars. It was a good buy so I grabbed them. Only problem was, they wouldn't run worth a nickel.

"Instead of throwing them away and admitting I'd been a sucker, I sold a couple. Both customers came back to complain. That's when I decided to throw them away before I made things worse. I should have been honest at first—but I learned.

"If you do something dumb, Charlie, put a stop to it before it gets worse."

"But what I did," Charlie argued, "wasn't really wrong—not at first anyway."

"I know what you mean, but it's easy to get carried away, isn't it?"

The door slammed loudly.

"Pete, what are you doing here?" Charlie asked.

"Just passing by. I have to take this bag of old clothes over to Mrs. Classen. Thought I'd pick up a candy bar first."

"What's happening at the house?"

"I'm not sure. The phone keeps ringing, and whenever Mom and Dad mention your name they look really mad."

"Are there any police there?"

"Of course not. Man, you seem worried."

"It's not that. I just need time to think. Will you do me a favor?"

"Depends."

"Will you stop at Mrs. Morgan's and see if Laura is there?"

"Sure—but I need nourishment." He grinned.

"All right, I'll buy you a candy bar. If you see Laura, tell her to meet me behind our shed."

"I want a Snickers."

Pete walked around to the back of the cottage looking for Mrs. Morgan. The door was open so he stepped inside.

Some noise came up from the basement, so Pete yelled down the stairs.

"Mrs. Morgan! Mrs. Morgan! Is Laura here?"

"Come on down, young man," Mrs. Morgan called.

Pete hesitated—he didn't want to stay long. But he hurried down the stairs.

"Over here, Pete."

Pete turned to his right and caught his breath. The pearl-handled pistol was three inches from his nose.

"Not one peep," Mrs. Morgan cautioned. "I'm not afraid to use this little sweetheart. Move over here."

Silently Pete followed Mrs. Morgan's command.

"Laura!" Pete exclaimed with shock.

"Mmmm, Mmmm," was all the tied and gagged girl could answer. Securely bound hand and foot, she sat on a chair.

"Sit here." Mrs. Morgan placed a chair next to Laura. Steadily she pointed her weapon at the nervous Pete.

"Why couldn't you kids leave me alone?" she muttered as she tied Pete's hands firmly behind him. A second rope was looped around his chest and knotted in the back.

"All I did was take a diamond away from some rich fat cats who didn't need it anyway." Pete's ankles were securely tied to the chair legs.

"Open your mouth," she ordered. Defiantly, Pete clamped his jaws as tightly as posible. "There is a cure for comedians," Mrs. Morgan warned. She lifted the revolver to Pete's temple and pulled the hammer back. His mouth instantly popped open.

"Kerry! Kerry!" Charlie yelled.

"I'm back here."

Kerry was sitting at a table on his back porch. A large apron covered his clothing and three heaping bushels of oysters were at his side.

"My mom said I should stay away from you," Kerry announced.

"She always says that. What did I do now?"

"My mom said that anyone who would sit on my lunch is no friend."

"Do you have to fix all these?"

"Yeah. I have to freeze some for later and clean the others for the refrigerator."

"That's too bad. If I was your friend I might be able to help you."

"That's a dirty trick, Charlie. There's another apron and a knife in the drawer."

"Which ones are which?" Charlie asked as he sat down.

"They've already been hosed down pretty well. Mom wants *all* of them shucked. She doesn't like to keep oysters in the shell."

"We're going to *shuck* all of these and bag 'em?" Charlie asked.

"You've got the right idea."

"Have you seen Laura? I can't find her anyplace."

"Not since school. But then, I don't look for her as

hard as you do," Kerry teased.

"And what does that mean?"

"You know what it means. I think you like that girl."

"Nuts to you."

"A lot of others think so, too."

"Do you see that oyster?" Charlie raised his voice. "Do you see that oyster?" He held the open shell in front of Kerry's nose. "That's what I think Laura looks like."

"Sure you do. Sure you do."

"I like Throckmorton more than I like her."

"Then why are you looking for her?"

"Because—because I have to talk to her, that's all. And I have to pretty soon."

Charlie scraped the oyster off its half shell and pushed its juice into the plastic bag. He tossed the shell into a basket.

Kerry pried another oyster open with a knife. Some shells opened easily but others held tightly.

"Tell me something honestly, Kerry."

"That's me—old honest Kerry."

"Do you think I would lie—I mean tell a real, hard, mean lie?"

"Well. . . ."

"What do you mean, 'well'?"

"Give me a second and I'll explain. You're just like Mrs. Warren in Biology. You ask me a question and then won't let me answer."

"Sometimes your kidding does get a little close to lying."

"Why, you rat," Charlie growled.

"Wait a minute." Kerry squeezed the plastic bag firmly together at the top to seal it. "All of us have trouble with it," Kerry continued. "We want to have fun and we get carried away."

"All right, big brain," Charlie interrupted. "How do you tell the difference between lying and kidding?"

"What do I know? It seems to me that if you're kidding, you don't hurt anyone—and you let the person know you *are* kidding. If you don't, it's probably a lie."

"And you think I do that?"

"You said it."

"Why you muskrat breath—"

"Don't get mad at me. You asked me. It just seems to me that since we've both become Christians, we ought to look a little closer at lying. Hey, I didn't bring this up, lunk-head, you did!"

"Even my friends are against me! Don't you have any idea where Laura could be?"

"Not one. She did talk a lot about Mrs. Morgan, so you might try there."

"I sent Pete over there but he hasn't gotten back. I doubt she'd be at Mrs. Morgan's."

"Haven't found a pearl yet," said Kerry as he zipped another bag shut.

"Me, either. Well, I'd better get out of here. Dad is going to skin me before the night's over."

Pete and Laura rolled their eyes at each other. Except for moans they had little communication. They could hear Mrs. Morgan walking about upstairs. They were sure she was packing to leave.

Terror filled them as they thought of the possibilities. Mrs. Morgan might come back with the gun and decide to silence them.

Refusing to give up easily, Pete surveyed the basement. To his left was an old wooden storage shelf. It held some canned goods left by the owner, but on the top shelf was a double-handled clay pot. Pete grinned at Laura as if he had the solution.

He nudged his shoulder against the shelf. It rocked slightly. Pete looked up to see if the pot had moved. It had. Only an inch or so, but it had moved. Pete smiled at Laura as much as the gag would allow him.

More roughly now, Pete bumped his shoulder against the wood. It tottered. Pete looked up; the pot was a little closer to the edge.

His idea was succeeding. When Mrs. Morgan returned to the basement, he would smash into the shelf and send the pot crashing onto her head. With her knocked out, they could cut themselves loose on the broken pottery and escape.

Pete knew it was a long shot, but he had to do something. She might return at any moment and shoot them.

Hope rose in Laura's heart as she realized what Pete had in mind. Silently she cheered him on.

It was tricky. If Pete hit the shelf too hard, Mrs. Morgan might hear the noise. If he didn't hit it hard enough, the pot wouldn't move.

Carefully he thrust his shoulder against the heavy board. The pot moved again. Pete gave it another bump. The pot jumped to the edge of the shelf. It began to rock back and forth as Pete and Laura watched anxiously. The pot refused to stop. It began rolling on its round base.

"Mmmm," was all Pete could groan as the pot tumbled off the ledge and crashed heavily on his head. Laura gave a muffled squeal as Pete slumped forward, unconscious.

Chapter Nine

"Maybe I should run over to Mrs. Morgan's," Charlie said as he opened the screen door. "My time is running out. I'll probably be shot by a firing squad at daybreak."

"Oops!" Kerry exclaimed as his calico cat ran between his legs. "Come back, Muffin, come back! Now I'm in trouble. My mom said I'd better not let that cat out again."

"Man, he can sure climb a tree," Charlie said.

"And me with a sprained ankle—I'll never get her down."

"I'd like to help, but I'm in too much trouble." Charlie started to leave.

"Go ahead, old buddy. What do you care if my mom breaks my neck?"

"You don't understand."

"It'll only take a couple of minutes to get her out of the tree. Come on, you owe it to me after nearly drowning me."

"I *what*?" Charlie said angrily.

"Sorry I mentioned it. Please?"

"Okay."

"Wait—I've got a good idea," Kerry announced. "I'll put my crutch through this basket handle and hold it up under the branch. Just scare Muffin and I'll catch her. We'll be done in no time."

Charlie obediently clambered up the tree while Kerry positioned himself under the limb.

"Here, kitty! Jump, Muffin, jump," Kerry called.

Charlie moved cautiously on his hands and knees.

"Just send her down, I'm ready. Jump, Muffin, jump."

Charlie's hand slipped on the branch.

"Hey!" he yelled as he lost his balance and swung under the limb. Fortunately his hands held tightly and he wrapped his legs around the branch. Charlie hung upside down like a koala bear.

"Are you all right?" Kerry asked.

"No problem. I can swing back on top."

Muffin stared at Charlie hanging upside down. She raced over to Charlie's clinging hands and began to dance with her claws on his helpless fingers.

"Aaah! Aaah!" Charlie screeched in pain.

"Muffin, back off," Kerry yelled.

The mischievous cat backed out toward the end of the limb. Resting her head on her paws, Muffin purred and seemed to grin.

Charlie pulled himself up and sat astraddle the branch. He looked at his scratched and stinging fingers.

"You're going to get it now," he warned the feline terror. Charlie inched his way closer.

Charlie purred at the cat. Muffin purred back.

"Don't let her scare you," warned Kerry.

Suddenly Muffin let out a terrifying yowl and leaped into the air. She landed wildly on Charlie's head. Her twitching tail brushed against Charlie's nose. Her claws dug painfully into his scalp.

"Off!" Charlie bellowed as Muffin's tail tickled his face.

"Here, kitty. Here, Muffin," Kerry called. He dropped his basket and reached for a stone. "Hold still, Charlie. I'll get her."

"Don't throw that—"

Klonk! The small stone bounced off the side of Charlie's head. Swish. A second one sailed past his chin.

Muffin held tightly. Each stone made her dig in deeper.

"Are you trying to kill me?" Charlie screamed.

"Don't move," Kerry insisted. "I'll get her this time."

"Move? How can I move?"

A third stone whistled through the air and smacked Charlie on the cheek. The bewildered cat jumped from Charlie's head and clung to the seat of Charlie's pants. Her sharp claws sank mercilessly into his skin.

Charlie wiggled desperately to dislodge the furry monster. Finally Muffin leaped to the ground below.

"You can't leave now," Kerry whined as Charlie hurried across the yard. Charlie's right hand held his head while his left rubbed the seat of his trousers.

"You ought to give that cat to the army as a new attack weapon."

"I've got to catch her," Kerry pleaded. "My mom—"

"Better yet. Give her to the artillery division and hope they shoot her out of a cannon."

Charlie left the yard huffing and groaning. Exasperated, Kerry gave up hobbling after his angry friend.

"Mrs. Morgan," Charlie called out as he knocked on her door.

"Oh, it's you," she replied approaching the doorway.

"May I come in?" Charlie asked.

"Well, I'm terribly busy right now," she objected.

"I won't take long." Charlie pushed his way inside.

His eye spotted a suitcase lying on the sofa.

"You aren't leaving so soon, are you?"

"Oh, no. Not for a couple more days," she lied. "I'm just getting my luggage out and checking it."

"Have you seen Laura? I can't find her anyplace."

"Not today." Mrs. Morgan's smile was warm, without a hint of deceit.

Charlie saw Laura's gym bag next to the end table. He pretended to ignore it.

"What about my brother, Pete?" he continued.

"My, no. I wish they would come by, though. I always enjoy seeing your friends."

"If you do see them, tell them I'm looking for them." Charlie excused himself and walked out the door. His mind raced to put the puzzle together. Maybe Laura had accidentally left her gym bag. But if she did, why would Mrs. Morgan lie about it? Things didn't seem right. He looked back. Mrs Morgan was walking toward her suitcase. He whirled and ran quietly to the side of the cottage. He carefully looked in each window. When he came to a basement window, he saw Laura and Pete helplessly tied to chairs.

There wasn't time to go for help. Charlie hurried to Mrs. Morgan's car. He crouched behind the vehicle for several seconds. There was a soft hissing sound. He gave a quick glance and ran toward the back door of the cottage. As quiet as a shadow Charlie turned the knob. He edged it open and nervously stepped inside. Charlie looked up toward the kitchen but saw no one. Stealthily he moved toward the basement staircase.

Charlie stopped and shivered. A piece of cold, silver metal was pressed against his neck.

"You should have gone home." Mrs. Morgan's voice was stiff, almost steel-like.

"That's a good idea. I'll do that right now."

"Not so fast, Charlie. Kids playing detective—someone could get hurt in this little game."

"If you'll excuse me, I have a dog who needs my love and support."

"Be quiet, you little fool. Go down the stairs—slowly. Put your hands up."

Charlie took each step very slowly as he tried to think of an escape plan.

"I'll tie you to this post."

The post was three feet away from Laura. Charlie's hands were bound behind him and his mouth was gagged with a strip torn from a dish towel.

Without another word Mrs. Morgan returned upstairs.

Charlie, Laura and Pete, having regained consciousness, looked at each other in silent desperation. They were afraid Mrs. Morgan would get away, or worse, that she might return with her revolver.

Charlie's eyes suddenly brightened as he noticed an oyster knife hanging on the shelf next to Laura. He winked and began to calculate.

With great effort Charlie swung his feet up, trying to knock the knife loose from its nail. Each time he hit the shelf it shook noisily.

Jars and pots jumped with each kick. One large jar tipped onto its side. The paraffin lid cracked and honey began to ooze out. Slowly the sweet, sticky liquid began to drip on Laura's head.

Charlie kept kicking. The knife bounced and jumped but would not fall.

Feeling her head grow wet, Laura turned her head up to look. A gooey stream of honey poured onto her face. She wiggled and squirmed but could not move out of the way. Her bound legs made it impossible to stand.

The honey kept cascading down. Soft, golden, goo poured over Laura's head and shoulders. The harder Charlie kicked, the more freely the honey poured from the jar. Laura's head and hair became soaked. Her shirt was shiny and sticky.

Charlie panted from exhaustion. Concentrating on putting all his energy into the kick, he again hurled his legs against the shelf.

Clink. The shucking knife hit the floor and skipped, bouncing toward Charlie. His tired legs reached and raked it closer. Charlie wiggled down toward the floor and turned around the post. His fingers stretched out and picked up the knife.

The old blade was rusty. Charlie sawed it awkwardly across the stiff rope. Each stroke made pressure and pain on his wrists.

Laura, moaning, stared at Charlie. Honey had snaked its way onto her jeans. Pete, still lightheaded, watched the two. A small cut crowned a red lump on his forehead.

Slam!

A door closed upstairs. Charlie sawed harder. Finally the rope fell from his wrists. As he pulled the gag from his mouth, he heard a car engine start.

Charlie quickly cut Pete loose. Then he hurried over to Laura and freed her.

"Swiss-cheese brain. Marshmallow head. Chicken-liver face," Laura angrily muttered when her mouth was freed. "You got honey all over me! And Mrs. Morgan got away!"

"Not yet," Charlie insisted with a grin. "I sabotaged her car—we can still catch her if we hurry."

The three scrambled up the stairs and bolted out the back door. There was only one direction in which Mrs. Morgan could escape. The other direction dead-ended at the Bay.

"Let's go," commanded Charlie. They began running down the highway.

"We're going to catch a car?" Pete exclaimed.

"Absolutely," Charlie yelled. "It's our only hope of catching Mrs. Morgan."

"I feel like a dog," said Laura—"chasing cars."

"You're no dog," Charlie reassured her. "I'd say you're a real *honey*."

Laura didn't smile. She kept trying to shake honey from her fingertips.

After a few hundred yards Pete began to pant heavily.

"How much farther?" he wheezed.

"Not much," Charlie gasped.

"What did you do to her car?" Laura asked.

"I let the air out of one of the tires. She'll have to stop at a gas station soon. Maybe she'll pull in to the one at the intersection."

They held their sides as they raced down the road. Pete began to lag behind.

"There it—there it—is." Charlie stopped and pointed to Mrs. Morgan's light blue Oldsmobile. An attendant was filling it with gas.

"Let's call the police," Laura said.

"We don't have time." Charlie was huffing like a steam engine. "She'll get away." He looked carefully. "She must be inside. Pete, you go in the back door. Laura and I will take the front."

"Watch out for that pistol," Laura cautioned.

"You got it, honey," Charlie teased.

When they reached the station, Charlie and Laura hunched down behind the cars. Bending down, Charlie scampered to Mrs. Morgan's car, reached through the open window and pulled the keys from the ignition. He tossed them across the parking area.

Laura then crawled along to the front door of the station. Carefully Charlie stooped by the opposite side of the door. Charlie nodded quickly. He and Laura burst through the doorway.

"Hold it!" Charlie shouted.

The station attendant and two customers turned in bewilderment. Laura and Charlie stood by the door, legs spread and hands raised as if ready to throw karate chops. Honey dripped from Laura's knees and ears.

"What's going on?" asked the attendant.

Pete darted through the back entrance holding a tire iron. "Freeze!" he shouted.

"Is this a junior high stunt or something?" asked one of the customers.

"She isn't here," Laura whispered.

"Quick, to the ladies' room—and grab one of the oil cans."

Laura and Charlie flanked the restroom door and readied themselves for trouble. Pete was close behind.

"This is very flattering," a soft voice came from behind them. "I don't often get this much attention."

They whirled to see Mrs. Morgan standing next to Pete. Her pearl-handled revolver was pointed at his temple.

"If Pete doesn't drop the tire iron, he is going to collect a new hole in his head." Her voice showed no sign of fear or uncertainty. Pete's weapon clanked on the concrete floor.

"We are going to walk slowly out the door and drive away. If no one bothers us or tries to follow, Pete will be dropped off down the road."

Everyone yielded a wide path as the two walked slowly toward the door.

Chapter Ten

Mrs. Morgan gripped the back of Pete's shirt as she eyed each person in the station. Carefully she backed out through the main door. The gun remained pressed against Pete's head.

"Around to the driver's side," Mrs. Morgan commanded.

Laura, hiding an oil can behind her back, circled slowly around the front of the car while Charlie moved around the back.

"Stay back!" the woman shouted.

Pete opened the car door and Mrs. Morgan pushed him across the driver's side. Laura threw the can at the woman's head. Mrs. Morgan swiveled and pointed her gun directly at Laura.

Charlie sprang like a tiger and lunged on Mrs. Morgan's back. He grabbed her weapon and lodged his fingers in the hammer. The lady seized Charlie's wrist and flipped him over her shoulder. He hit the pavement with a grunt.

Mrs. Morgan turned and ran behind the station. She was running down the hill behind the building as the three rounded the back of the station.

"Hold it!" Charlie warned his two friends. "If we chase her she could blast us. This'll work better."

Reaching for an empty oil barrel, Charlie laid the

drum on its side. With one great thrust he sent it rolling down the hill. They stood nervously watching it pick up speed.

Bonk! The barrel bounced into Mrs. Morgan's legs and threw her into the air. As she became airborne, the pearl-handled revolver dropped from her hand.

When Charlie, Laura and Pete arrived, the disheveled Mrs. Morgan was still lying flat on the ground. Charlie and Laura pulled her arms behind her back and tied her wrists with Charlie's belt. They helped her to her feet.

Pete retrieved the pistol and pointed it at the crook.

"Don't try anything," he barked.

"Oh, don't be foolish," Mrs. Morgan insisted. "There aren't any bullets in that gun. If there had been, you kids would have been done for."

"You mean you would have *shot* us?" Laura asked.

"Of course not. That's why I didn't buy any bullets."

Police sirens were wailing in the distance. Soon red lights were flashing everywhere.

"Why in the world would a nice lady like you steal diamonds?" Charlie asked.

"Just for something to do. When Mr. Morgan died, I was left alone. I had never done anything exciting in all my life. That's when I started stealing diamonds. This was my fourth big one. Who'd ever suspect a little old lady?"

"Couldn't you crochet or join a garden club?" Laura wondered.

"Diamonds sound more interesting, don't you agree?"

The police escorted Mrs. Morgan to a patrol car. They wrapped her gun in a bag as evidence.

"Oh, no!" Charlie exclaimed with a moan. "Now I have to go home and explain this to my dad."

The next day Charlie, Laura, Pete and Mr. and Mrs. Dean were sitting in the office of Police Chief Olson.

"This has to be one of the strangest stories I have ever heard," said the bewildered chief. "You mean you guys knew all along that Mrs. Morgan was the diamond thief?"

"Well, we kind of did," Pete explained.

"We knew about the chocolate marshmallows," said Laura, "but we weren't sure that she'd actually hidden the diamond in them."

"Wouldn't it have been better to let the police in on that bit of information?" the chief asked.

"We wanted to," Charlie explained, "but we were afraid you wouldn't believe us."

"Frankly, young man, we still aren't sure we believe you. This tale about the marshmallows is a hard one to swallow. Our men have gone through the candy in Laura's gym bag and didn't find a diamond."

Pete gulped. "You didn't?"

"You mean Mrs. Morgan *isn't* a diamond thief?" Mrs. Dean asked.

"We can't find the diamond. She has confessed but only because she thinks we have it."

"Don't be worried, folks," Charlie announced. "I have the diamond." He pulled a crumpled piece of cloth out of his pocket and unwrapped it. The beautiful Ludlow Diamond glistened in the light.

"How did you get it?" Laura asked.

"That was easy. When I went back over to visit the second time, I was able to get into the candy. She didn't watch me as closely that time. The third piece I picked up had the diamond."

"You let me go over there when you *knew* she was the diamond thief?" Laura growled. "You're lower than a lizard. You almost got me killed!"

"I couldn't decide what to do. I was hoping she would leave. She was such a nice old lady. I didn't want to see her go to jail. And since I had the diamond, I figured the problem was solved."

"No matter how nice she is, she can't go around stealing diamonds," the Chief said sternly.

"You kids aren't the best detectives in the world," he continued. "In fact, I'd be tempted to say you are downright dangerous. However, I'm going to recommend all three of you for the Bay Citizenship Award. Whether you kids are brave or stupid, you deserve it."

A couple of weeks later Charlie and Laura were again out on the water. It was colder now but still good weather for tonging oysters.

Charlie dipped his long-handled tongs into the water and probed for dark shells. Laura ran her heavy tongs along the bottom.

"I didn't think your dad was ever going to let you out again," Laura said.

"Grounding me is his favorite punishment. He says it proves he really cares for me," Charlie admitted. "People called our house for days, even though the newspaper said my photo was a hoax. Even Dad's cousin in St. Louis saw the picture and called. It was everywhere."

"How did the papers get it?" Laura raised her

tongs and dumped a load of oysters on the bottom of the boat.

"Someone picked it up on the police desk and ran it to the newspaper office. No one asked permission or anything."

"I never even mention the monster anymore." Laura sifted through her catch. "People only laugh at me."

"What do you think we actually saw that evening?" Charlie wondered.

"Hard to tell. The best thing for us to do is forget about it. If we bring it up anymore, they're going to ship us off to the funny farm."

"You're right. I think I'll save it and probably tell my grandchildren. I s'pose they won't believe me either."

"Charlie! CHARLIE!"

Silently a round green head with white eyes and jagged teeth came swimming toward them.